Morris GLEITZMAN

Worm Story

PUFFIN

PUFFIN BOOKS

Published by the Penguin Group
Penguin Books Ltd, 80 Strand, London WC2R 0RL, England
Penguin Group (USA) Inc., 375 Hudson Street, New York, New York 10014, USA
Penguin Group (Canada), 10 Alcorn Avenue, Toronto, Ontario, Canada M4V 3B2
(a division of Pearson Penguin Canada Inc.)
Penguin Ireland, 25 St Stephen's Green, Dublin 2, Ireland (a division of Penguin Books Ltd)
Penguin Group (Australia), 250 Camberwell Road, Camberwell, Victoria 3124, Australia
(a division of Pearson Australia Group Pty Ltd)
Penguin Books India Pvt Ltd, 11 Community Centre,
Panchsheel Park, New Delhi – 110 017, India
Penguin Group (NZ), cnr Airborne and Rosedale Roads, Albany,
Auckland 1310, New Zealand (a division of Pearson New Zealand Ltd)
Penguin Books (South Africa) (Pty) Ltd, 24 Sturdee Avenue,
Rosebank, Johannesburg 2196, South Africa

Penguin Books Ltd, Registered Offices: 80 Strand, London WC2R 0RL, England

www.penguin.com

First published in Australia by Penguin Group (Australia),
a division of Pearson Australia Group Pty Ltd 2004
First published in Great Britain in Puffin Books 2005

3

Text copyright © Creative Input Pty Ltd, 2004
Illustrations copyright © Simon Bosch, 2004
All rights reserved

The moral right of the author and illustrator has been asserted

Set in Minion
Made and printed in England by Clays Ltd, St Ives plc

British Library Cataloguing in Publication Data
A CIP catalogue record for this book is available from the British Library

ISBN 0–141–32018–4

www.greenpenguin.co.uk

Penguin Books is committed to a sustainable future
for our business, our readers and our planet.
The book in your hands is made from paper
certified by the Forest Stewardship Council.

PUFFIN BOOKS

Worm Story

Morris Gleitzman was born and educated in England, but lives in Australia. He has worked as a paperboy, a frozen chicken de-froster and an assistant to a fashion designer, but he is best known for his hugely successful children's books. He's had tummy worms three times, head lice heaps, and he is currently the proud host to 12,873,654,927,063 microbes. He doesn't know all their names yet.

Visit Morris at his website:
www.morrisgleitzman.com

For
Jean McFadyen

Just before the huge storm rolled down the valley, Wilton did.

It wasn't his fault.

He was on a ledge high over the valley doing his exercises. Or trying to.

'One push-up,' Wilton grunted. 'Two push-ups. Three push-ups.'

It was no good. He wasn't moving.

Wilton flopped forward onto his tummy.

This is hopeless, he thought. I'll never lose weight this way.

'You'll never lose weight that way,' said a nearby patch of slime, looking up at Wilton with the know-it-all expression patches of slime are famous for. 'Push-ups don't work when you haven't got any tendrils to push yourself up with.'

'Thanks for the advice,' said Wilton.

'What you need,' said the patch of slime, 'is to find the right exercise for your particular physique.'

The slime's right, thought Wilton. There must be one workout suitable for a very large tube-shaped limbless microbe like me. Something that doesn't involve push-ups, jogging or cartwheels.

He tried to think of it.

All he could come up with was wriggling.

OK, thought Wilton. If all I can do is wriggle, I'm going to wriggle like I've never wriggled before.

He gave it a go.

'Wow,' said the patch of slime. 'Great wriggling.'

Wilton's wriggles were so powerful and determined that before he knew it he'd done a complete lap of the ledge and was back where he started. Skidding, he saw to his horror, onto the patch of slime.

'Oof,' grunted the patch of slime. 'You haven't lost any weight so far.'

Before he could apologise, Wilton found himself skidding off the patch of slime, off the entire ledge, and falling, bouncing, rolling down into the valley.

Oh no, he thought. Now I'm in big trouble.

'Look out,' he yelled.

Farm-worker microbes flung themselves out of his path, waving their plasma strands in panic. So did livestock. Flocks of viruses bolted. Herds of enzymes cowered together.

Somehow, as Wilton rolled and bounced his way through them, he managed not to crush a single one. The only things he squashed were some of his own front molecules when he came to a sudden stop in a paddock of sludge.

'Sorry,' he mumbled to the livestock and the farm workers and his front molecules as he wriggled backwards out of the sludge.

'I should hope you are,' said a gruff voice.

Wilton winced.

Glaring up at him, squiz molecules bulging, tendrils on hips, was a tiny frowning blob, wrinkled all over with age and indignation.

Oh no, a farmer.

'What are you doing here?' growled the farmer.

Wilton resisted the temptation to say anything smarty cells like 'trying to lose weight'.

'Well?' demanded the farmer.

'Um,' said Wilton. 'I slipped.'

The ancient farmer scowled. 'Stop me if there's anything you don't understand about the following,' he said. 'Our world consists of a valley bottom, where we are now, and the valley slopes up there, where you are meant to stay. Sound familiar?'

Wilton nodded sadly.

'Good,' continued the farmer. 'Because there are very important reasons why you're not allowed down here, aren't there?'

'Yes,' said Wilton quietly. 'When I come down here it terrifies the livestock and gives them headaches.'

In the sludge paddocks and along the banks of the sludge river, the viruses and enzymes were still whimpering nervously and some were rubbing their ectoplasms.

'That's one reason,' said the farmer.

'They're only frightened of me because they don't know me,' said Wilton. 'Let me stay down here and help out for a while. Do a bit of sludge grooming. Fence a few sludge paddocks. I can make friends down here, I know I can.'

The farmer narrowed his squiz molecules and scratched his grizzled ectoplasm with a work-calloused tendril.

'Please,' begged Wilton. 'I'm lonely up there on the slopes. Let me be a farm worker.'

Wilton's hope molecules were buzzing. So were his fear molecules. Blurting out his life's ambition to the gruffest farmer in the valley was one of the scariest things he'd ever done.

The farmer squinted up at him in silence.

Wilton knew this wasn't a good sign. He hoped the farmer was just pausing to digest his lunch, but when Wilton peeked into the farmer's protoplasm he couldn't make out a single virus kebab or enzyme nugget.

'You've already got one big problem, lad,' growled the farmer at last. 'Don't be an idiot as well. You know why we can't have you down here.'

'Why?' asked Wilton, even though he was pretty sure he knew.

'Because,' said the farmer wearily, 'you're too fat.'

'That's right,' said several muffled voices. 'Way too fat.'

Indignation molecules vibrated inside Wilton. It

was a painful feeling because, as Wilton was the first to admit, he had a lot of indignation molecules. He had a lot of every type of molecule. That was the problem.

'I'm not fat,' said Wilton to the farmer. 'I'm just big.'

'Way too big,' said the muffled voices.

'Fat, big, whatever,' said the farmer. 'Modern sludge farming is an exact and demanding science. I can't have great lumps like you flobbing around the place squashing crops and workers.'

'I haven't squashed any workers for ages,' protested Wilton.

'You're doing it now,' said the farmer.

'That's right,' said the muffled voices.

Wilton felt something tickling under his tummy. He wriggled backwards. A few hundred flattened microbes picked themselves up and tried to push their ectoplasms back into shape. Wilton felt awful. The round ones were sort of oval now, and most of the stick-shaped ones were crinkled.

'Sorry,' said Wilton, wishing he had tendrils so he could help straighten them out.

'We don't want to hear sorry, fatso,' said one of the squashed workers. 'We just want to hear you're on a diet.'

Wilton felt shame molecules burning inside him.

'I am on a diet,' he replied. 'All I've eaten for ages is a bit of water membrane and a few dried viruses with the skin off.'

'Well,' grunted the farmer, peering up at Wilton, 'it's not working.'

Wilton wanted to let the farmer know that he was also doing an exercise programme. But before he could get the words out, he felt more tickling under his tummy. For a moment he thought more workers were still under there, flapping desperately.

Then he realised it was something else.

The ground was vibrating.

Wilton knew what that meant.

'A storm's coming,' he said urgently to the farmer.

Already Wilton could feel a wet breeze against his skin. The farmer peered down the valley and Wilton saw his ancient tendrils stiffen with alarm.

'Storm,' yelled the farmer. 'Take cover.'

Chaos broke out.

Workers flung themselves in all directions. Livestock stampeded. Enzymes desperately clung to the backs of viruses while the viruses tried to hide behind the enzymes.

Wilton did what he always did when he was caught out in a storm. He curled into a circle, partly to brace himself against the impact of the wind, partly to give some of the farm workers and livestock a place in the middle to shelter.

The storm hit with a roaring squelch.

It was the worst one Wilton could remember. The rain was lashing harder than ever before. It stung Wilton even more than the squashed workers' unkind comments.

The ground heaved under Wilton's belly as if the whole valley floor had been infected with a puke fungus.

The howling wind was so savage it tore lumps of sludge from the rippling sludge fields and flung them about like . . . Wilton didn't know what they were like. He'd never seen anything as big as the lumps that were splodging onto the ground all around him.

'Fat boy,' yelled the farmer, huddled under an old raincoat made of dead plasma strands and matted whiskers.

Wilton knew the farmer was yelling at him.

'When this is over,' continued the farmer, 'get back up that slope and stay there. If I see you down here again, making the sludge gods angry like this, you'll be a very sorry microbe.'

Wilton didn't reply.

He just stayed curled up.

The storm was bad, but it was nothing compared to how miserable he felt inside.

'Be honest with me,' Wilton said to the neighbours. 'Am I fat?'

The neighbours didn't reply.

Wilton knew why. The neighbours always found it hard to speak when they were jammed between their cave wall and his bottom.

He shifted to give them a bit of space. It wasn't easy. Less than half a wriggle and now Wilton was squashed against the ceiling.

'Fat?' said one of the neighbours as soon as she had room for her chat molecules to vibrate. 'Don't be silly, you're not fat, not really. Our cave's a bit small, that's all.'

'More of a crevice than a cave,' said the other neighbour.

Wilton gave them both a grateful squiz.

He was lucky to have such nice blood cells as neighbours, but he knew they weren't being completely honest with him. Their cave wasn't small. Compared to other places Wilton had seen, it was massive. Without him here clogging it up, the neighbours could be holding an afternoon tea for a very large number of corpuscles.

It's me, thought Wilton sadly. I'm too big.

And getting bigger.

That was the really worrying thing. One more growth spurt and even his friendly neighbours wouldn't want him to visit.

'Did you pop in for a reason?' said the first neighbour. 'If you're hoping to borrow some cleaning products to mop up after the storm, I'm afraid our enzymes are all busy.'

'Thanks,' said Wilton, 'but I've already cleaned up my ledge.'

'What is it, then?' said the other neighbour. 'We don't want to rush you but we're a bit busy too.'

Wilton fired up every one of his courage molecules.

'You know how I haven't got any parents?' he said.

The neighbours nodded.

'You've told us several times,' said one. 'You've never had any and you've searched the whole valley and you haven't found a single sign of any.'

'Very sad,' said the other.

'Extremely sad,' said the first. 'Was that all?'

Wilton's chat molecules were so tense he could hardly get the words out.

'I was wondering,' he said, 'if you'd adopt me.'

The neighbours stared at him, their squiz molecules bulging.

'It's OK,' continued Wilton hurriedly. 'I'd stay up the slope on my ledge. I wouldn't bother you or squash you. It's just that I wouldn't feel so lonely if I knew I had a mum and dad. And if the folk down in the valley knew I was a member of a respectable family, they might be a bit friendlier to me.'

The neighbours were staring at each other and Wilton had a horrible feeling he could see panic in their squiz molecules. They were both looking very red, even for red blood cells.

'Trouble is,' said the first neighbour, 'we're just so busy. I'm doing shift work in the spleen.'

'And I've got clients I have to visit in the kidneys,' said the other neighbour. 'And the liver.'

'It's a mess in that spleen,' said the first neighbour. 'We're all on overtime.'

Wilton didn't know where these places were, but he knew what the neighbours were saying.

No.

There was an awkward silence.

Wilton gave it one more try.

'Could you be my aunty and uncle then?'

From the neighbours' grim expressions, Wilton saw they didn't like that idea either. His hope molecules sagged.

'Wouldn't work,' said the first neighbour, her chat molecules vibrating with fake regret. 'We're blood corpuscles and you're a microbe.'

'Not only that,' said the other neighbour. 'You're a very fat microbe.'

Wilton lay on his ledge, staring down into the valley.

Far below, the vast sludge river glowed as it moved slowly through the paddocks. Wilton's whiff molecules could just pick up its faint but fragrant perfume.

The folk down in the valley were too far away for Wilton to see what they were doing, but if he strained his noise molecules he could hear faint but happy voices and the occasional popping sound.

'Whatever they're doing,' murmured Wilton, 'it sounds like fun.'

Microbes being friendly.

Caring about each other.

'Don't torture yourself,' said the patch of slime next to Wilton on the ledge. 'We're outcasts. Accept it.'

Wilton turned away from the valley.

'You're right,' he said.

Oh well, at least he had the patch of slime to keep him company.

'And now you've accepted it,' said the patch of slime, 'get back over to your side of the ledge. I don't want you squashing me again. Just my luck to be sharing a ledge with the bulgiest wriggliest heaviest microbe in the whole world.'

'It's not my fault,' said Wilton. 'I wish I was like the others. Tiny and popular.'

'Well you're not,' said the patch of slime. 'So nick off.'

Wilton didn't nick off. His loneliness molecules were aching and he needed to talk.

'I just wish I knew why I'm so different,' he said. 'Apart from being too big, I haven't got any tendrils or plasma strands. All the other microbes have. Everyone in the valley's got something they can do push-ups with except me.'

'Hey,' snapped the patch of slime. 'If you think you've got it bad, take a squiz at me. Those sludge gods really cheated me. When I was a little patch of slime I dreamed of being a patrol officer in the immune system. Whizzing around the valley blasting fungus and handing out parking tickets. Look at me. I can't even wriggle.'

'You're right,' said Wilton quietly. 'I'm sorry. I'm not the only one with problems.'

'Those sludge gods,' said the patch of slime bitterly. 'OK, they give us the precious sludge that nourishes our valley, but in their infinite wisdom they really give some of us the rough end of the enzyme.'

'Yes,' said Wilton. 'They do.'

'Now go away,' said the patch of slime. 'You're giving me a headache.'

Wilton wriggled over to the other side of the ledge.

He felt so lonely he wished he could hug himself, but he couldn't, not until he grew some hugging equipment.

Will that ever happen? he wondered sadly as he gazed up at the vast pink vein-threaded sky.

Will I ever know why I'm so different?

Suddenly Wilton realised what he had to do.

The thought sent his fear molecules into a frenzy, but then his determination molecules took over.

It was clear as blood plasma.

There was only one way to discover the truth about himself.

'Excuse me,' said Wilton, wriggling out from behind a pimple. 'Do you know where I can find the sludge gods?'

He felt pretty confident asking farm workers. They'd probably know because they worked with sludge all the time.

On the valley slope the farm workers looked up, startled to see him, their plasma strands flapping.

'Actually,' said Wilton. 'Just one sludge god would do.'

'Don't waste your energy, fatso,' replied one of the workers. 'We've been waiting for a sign from the sludge gods ever since the storm, to find out why they're punishing us. We've been grovelling, wailing, beseeching, sacrificing enzymes, you name it. Nothing.'

'Perhaps they prefer a more personal approach,' said Wilton. 'Like a visit.'

The farm workers stared at him as if he was

one think molecule short of an intelligent life-form. Wilton could see their squiz molecules overheating.

'Are you bonkers?' said another worker. 'Nobody has ever visited the sludge gods. Not in the history of the whole valley.'

'I thought I might,' said Wilton.

'Have your think molecules gone for a stroll in that big fat body of yours and got lost?' said a third worker. 'The sludge gods are angry. They're furious. You don't want to go anywhere near them when they're in this mood.'

Wilton found himself hoping the workers weren't sludge god experts after all.

'How do you know they're angry?' said Wilton. 'The storms might be caused by something else.'

'Look at the sludge,' said another worker. 'The sludge only goes like this when the gods are angry.'

Wilton peered at the huge lump of storm-tossed sludge the workers were clearing up. He had to admit it didn't look too good. Its usual bright colours were dull and dingy. The jagged orange fragments that the ancient legends called carrot were more of a dirty yellow. The green chunks the legends called peas were closer to grey.

Perhaps the workers are right, thought Wilton. Perhaps the sludge gods are angry.

He pushed the thought out of his molecules and started back up the slope.

'When I've asked the sludge gods why I'm

different,' Wilton called down to the workers, 'I'll also ask them why the sludge is off colour.'

'We can tell you why you're different,' yelled the first worker. 'It's because you're fat.'

'But you won't be for much longer if you go pestering the sludge gods,' yelled the second worker. 'They'll grind you into sludge.'

Wilton had never wriggled this far in his life, not even when he was looking for parents.

His whole body was sore. The skin on his belly was sorest. He tried rolling over and wriggling on his back, but that just made his back skin sore too.

Oh well, thought Wilton. At least I've left the farm workers behind.

Nobody had called him fatso for ages.

That was one good thing.

One not-so-good thing was that the valley down this end was more of a narrow chasm. The sludge flowed much faster here and the valley slopes were very steep. Wilton had to wriggle along the upper slopes very carefully in case he lost his balance and rolled down into the surging river of sludge.

He didn't fancy that. As well as flowing scarily fast, the river was giving off a musty sour smell. Wilton could just make out the enzymes that usually frolicked and played happily in the sludge. They were lying listlessly on the fast-moving surface with the faded lumps of carrot and peas.

Wilton paused to rest his aching ectoplasm.

'Excuse me,' he said to a passing speck of fungus. 'Do you know if any sludge gods live around here?'

The fungus didn't reply.

'I thought if I followed the sludge it would lead me to them,' said Wilton. 'The ancient legends say that the sludge comes to us from the sludge gods and flows back to the sludge gods. I think it's called the enchanted circle of sludge. But I haven't seen a single god and I'll probably be back where I started soon.'

'Don't tell me your problems, fatso,' said the fungus, not even stopping. 'I've got a migraine like you wouldn't believe.'

That's strange, thought Wilton as he wriggled on. The farm workers and livestock have been getting headaches lately too. And at least one very grumpy farmer. That's something else I'll have to ask the sludge gods about if I ever find them.

Wilton rounded a bend in the valley and stopped. All thoughts of headaches vanished from his think molecules. His squiz molecules struggled to take in what was in front of him.

The end of the valley.

This is impossible, thought Wilton. The valley can't just end.

But it did. A few wriggles ahead of him the valley slopes vanished. So did the sludge river.

And now Wilton's noise molecules were picking up a distant roaring sound.

He wriggled forward, dizzy, confused, trying to work out how the valley could just stop.

Then he saw how.

The valley dropped away in a sheer cliff.

The sludge was flowing over the edge of the cliff, the thundering roar mingling with the alarmed squeaks of plummeting enzymes.

Wilton lay trembling at the very edge of the cliff, at the very edge of the known world, and peered down at what he was pretty sure no microbe had ever seen before.

Another valley.

It couldn't be.

It was.

As Wilton gazed down, his fear molecules gave a jolt and his think molecules snapped out of their shock.

This had to be the sludge gods' valley. That's why it was protected by a huge sheer cliff. Important individuals like sludge gods wouldn't want to be pestered by crowds of whingeing farmers queueing up to complain about the weather and herds of gossiping farm workers dropping in to ask advice about their holidays. They'd want peace and quiet to make wise decisions.

Wilton's fear molecules danced around inside him.

He couldn't see any sludge gods. But they could be anywhere. Down there. Or over there. Glaring angrily up at him. Getting ready to grind him into sludge.

Suddenly Wilton wondered if going to see the sludge gods was such a good idea.

He wriggled away from the edge of the cliff.

Maybe I'll just go back, he thought. Life on my ledge at home isn't so bad. There are worse things than everyone calling me fatso and not wanting to be my friend.

Being ground into sludge was one of them.

But not knowing the truth was one of them too.

Wilton went back to the edge of the cliff.

'Excuse me, your sludge godlinesses,' he yelled down into the depths of the valley. 'Can I ask you a couple of questions?'

Wilton waited for the sludge gods to reply.

Nothing.

Not even a little sludge storm to show they were listening but a bit irritated.

Wilton didn't give up.

'I was just wondering, your sludge godlinesses,' he yelled, 'why I'm so huge and different and possibly fat. I'm also wondering if I'll be like this for the rest of my life, or whether it's just a stage I'm going through. If I'll grow out of it and end up the same size as all the other microbes, please give me a sign now.'

Wilton waited, hope molecules doing nervous cartwheels inside him.

Nothing.

Come on, thought Wilton. Fair go. At least answer my questions.

19

'Please,' he yelled down into the sludge gods' valley. 'I'm desperate.'

'I can see that,' said a voice behind him. 'Which question would you like me to answer first?'

Wilton spun round so quickly he almost fell off the cliff.

He would have dropped to his knees if he had knees. If he had tendrils he would have dropped to those. As it was, his tummy was already on the ground, so he just sort of sagged a bit in reverence.

Then he saw he didn't have to.

It wasn't a sludge god revealing itself to him there on the clifftop, it was a microbe crawling out from under an upside-down boat.

Wilton stared.

Jeepers, he thought. What a tiny microbe. And what a weird round boat.

The microbe didn't seem the slightest bit worried by its lack of size, not judging by the way it was standing there cockily with its tendrils outstretched.

'Forget those dopey sludge gods,' said the microbe. 'Because have I got some big answers for you.'

Wilton wriggled back, careful not to flop over

the cliff. It was tragic. He'd seen this sort of thing before. A microbe so tiny it didn't have enough think molecules to keep a grip on reality.

'No offence,' said Wilton to the microbe. 'But this is private.'

He waited for the microbe to leave.

It didn't.

'Don't get your molecules in a knot, Wriggles,' said the microbe. 'You can trust me. I won't tell a cell.'

Wilton drew himself up to his full height, and width, and length, looming over the microbe.

'When I say private,' said Wilton sternly, 'I mean just me.'

The microbe took a step back and drew itself up to its full height, which wasn't much different from before except its tendrils were trembling nervously.

'You're not scaring me,' said the microbe.

Wilton gave it an even sterner glare.

'OK, you are a bit,' said the microbe.

It scurried back under its strange round boat, and started tottering down towards the river with it. The boat was many times larger than the microbe and only the microbe's lower tendrils were visible.

Wilton started to feel concerned.

If the little tyke fell into the sludge torrent with that thing, both would be swept over the edge.

'Wait,' said Wilton wearily. 'What was it you wanted to tell me?'

The microbe stopped and scrambled out from under the boat.

'OK,' it said, spreading its tendrils. 'Are you ready for this? It's a biggie, so prepare yourself.'

'Just say it,' said Wilton.

'You're a worm,' said the microbe.

Wilton stared, wondering if the microbe was calling him names, which would have been a bit unfair seeing as he was trying to save the little dope's ectoplasm.

The microbe didn't look like it was name-calling. It was grinning at Wilton with the expression of someone who'd just delivered very good news.

'A worm?' said Wilton. 'What's a worm?'

'It's a type of species,' said the microbe. 'Your species.'

Wilton digested this for a long time. His think molecules started to buzz with excitement.

Of course.

This explains everything.

Why I'm so long and wriggly and heavily built.

Why I've always found it so hard to make friends with microbes.

I'm a different species.

I'm a worm.

Wilton was trembling himself now, with emotion.

Then he remembered there was every possibility this microbe didn't have two think molecules to rub together and was spouting gibberish.

Wilton turned away from the grinning microbe, confused. And saw, in the sludge river below,

23

speeding towards the cliff, lots more long wriggly heavily built creatures just like him.

'Hey,' yelled Wilton as he slithered frantically down to the edge of the river. 'Hang on, I want to talk to you.'

Most of the worms had already disappeared over the cliff in the torrent of sludge. Wilton wrapped his tail round a small pimple, curved the rest of his body out over the river and managed to hook it under one of the worms. The creature was almost as big as him, and Wilton nearly sprained his back dragging the worm onto the riverbank.

He didn't care about the pain and the possible permanent injury.

This was what he'd dreamed of for as long as he could remember.

A friend just like himself.

Wilton gently scraped the sludge off the worm's body. He decided to give it a few moments to recover before he introduced himself.

Well, a couple of moments.

'G'day,' he said. 'I'm Wilton.'

The worm didn't reply. Or move.

'Are you hurt?' asked Wilton softly.

Already he was planning all the fun things he and his new friend could do together once the new friend had rested and recovered.

The worm still didn't move. Or say anything.

'Wriggles,' said another voice nearby. 'Sorry to interrupt, but . . .'

It was the microbe, who'd staggered down the slope with the boat.

'Not just now,' said Wilton. 'I'm grateful for everything you've done for me, but I just want some time with my new friend if that's OK.'

'That's what I'm trying to . . .' squeaked the microbe.

'Shhhh,' said Wilton and turned back to the worm, who still wasn't moving.

Oh no.

Wilton couldn't see a flicker of life. Not a squiz twitch or an ectoplasm ripple or anything.

'Don't die,' he whispered desperately to the worm. 'Please don't die. I've got a great ledge we can play on. Hang on. Please.'

Wilton wished he knew how to do mouth-to-mouth. He'd seen it done on some half-drowned bacteria. Except this worm didn't seem to have a food tube. Or, come to that, squiz molecules.

'It's not a worm,' said the microbe.

Wilton stopped staring at where the worm's food tube should be, and stared at the microbe.

'But it's exactly the same shape as me,' he said. 'And you just told me I'm a worm.'

'It's a noodle,' said the microbe.

'A noodle?' said Wilton.

Disappointment molecules flooded through him in sickening waves. He remembered he'd heard an ancient legend about noodles once. Something about curry sauce, whatever that was. The legend

25

had described how noodles were long and wriggly and heavily built.

A horrible thought hit Wilton.

What if I'm a noodle too? Does that mean one day my food tube will grow over and my squiz molecules will shrink to nothing and I'll end up flopped on the ground, lifeless and sauceless?

Wilton pushed the thought out of his molecules.

'I'm not listening to you any more,' he said to the microbe. 'You're not a worm expert, you're a loony.'

'I never said I was an expert,' said the microbe. 'I just know that worms look like you and they hatch out of these.'

The microbe tapped the hull of the round boat.

'Worms hatch out of boats?' said Wilton.

He couldn't believe he was still having this conversation.

'Not boats,' said the microbe. 'Eggs.'

The microbe flipped the boat over so Wilton could see inside it.

'When your egg arrived at our place,' continued the microbe, 'and you hatched out, we were amazed. We'd never seen anything like it. When you nicked off so quickly I thought you knew you were a worm. Until I heard you yelling to the farm workers about visiting the sludge gods. Then I realised I'd better fill you in.'

Wilton stared at the microbe.

Could this be true?

He remembered the microbe was a loony. A kind loony, but a loony.

Wilton was about to thank the microbe and say a very firm goodbye when suddenly a strange feeling rippled through him and he found he couldn't stop staring at the boat.

The more he looked, the stronger the feeling became.

Perhaps I'm the mental one, thought Wilton. I've got an overpowering urge to curl up inside a strange boat that's about a hundred times too small for me.

He wriggled closer.

His whiff molecules were picking up a faint aroma among the smells of sludge and microbe. A forgotten, familiar aroma.

Wilton trembled at the memory.

The ground started trembling too, but Wilton hardly noticed it.

He stared at the dried membrane on the interior of the egg shell. As he did, a wet breeze hit his skin. For a fleeting moment, the feeling of moisture all around him was as familiar as the smell.

Then suddenly the breeze wasn't a breeze any more, it was a wind.

Wilton flung himself towards the microbe.

'Storm,' he yelled. 'Take cover.'

The microbe squeaked with alarm and pulled the egg on top of itself.

Wilton curled around them both.

The screaming wind slammed into them so hard that Wilton felt himself being blown out straight again. Worse, he was being blown towards the edge of the cliff.

'Hang on,' he yelled at the microbe. But the egg was gone. So was the microbe.

Desperately, Wilton pressed himself into the clifftop. His tail was out over the void, flapping from side to side in the gale. Near his shoulder he could hear the sludge thundering over the cliff, driven even faster by the wind.

Wilton knew he had a very important decision to make.

He could struggle with all his might and hang on till the storm was over. Then he could go back to his lonely ledge and forget he'd ever heard the words 'egg' and 'worm'.

That would be the safe and sensible thing to do.

Or he could take a risk that the microbe was right. He could continue his journey into the unknown and if he was lucky and didn't get mulched by the sludge gods he could meet some other worms and if he was even luckier he could make a friend his own size who wasn't a noodle.

That would be the dangerous and crazy thing to do.

It was a hard decision.

Once Wilton had made it, though, continuing his journey was easy. He just let go of the clifftop and the wind hurled him down into the valley of the sludge gods.

Wilton's plan, when he let go of the clifftop, was to wrap himself around a big soft chunk of plummeting sludge and let that break his fall at the bottom.

Bad plan, he soon realised.

The wind was too strong. The sludge was too slippery.

'Tendrils,' wailed Wilton as he spun downwards. 'Why wasn't I born with tendrils?'

'I know how you feel,' said a plummeting enzyme clinging to a lump of sludge. 'I always wanted bigger molecules.'

Molecules.

The word filled Wilton with terror.

Because suddenly he found himself thinking about what would happen when he and the sludge got to the bottom of the cliff. He wasn't sure of all the details, but it would probably involve the sludge slamming into the valley floor with such force that it would explode into its separate molecules.

Him too.

Wilton was very fond of his molecules. He liked them to be happy, but having them wandering off doing their own thing was not good.

Wilton struggled to curl himself into a tight ball.

He glanced fearfully down at the valley floor, bracing himself for the shattering impact.

But it didn't happen.

That's a relief, thought Wilton.

Then he realised why the impact hadn't happened.

He and the sludge were plummeting into the dark gaping mouth of a huge tunnel in the valley floor.

The tunnel was already half full of sludge, and the force of the plummet flung Wilton deep into its sludgy depths. He bumped against what felt like lumps of carrot and chunks of peas and other things he half-remembered hearing about in ancient sludge legends.

Popcorn and pizza and watermelon and sausages and possibly custard.

He wasn't sure exactly what custard was, but he was pretty sure it was sharp, which meant this could be custard now, jabbing him in the neck.

Wilton wriggled back to the surface just in time for more arriving splodges of sludge to bury him again. Bruised and battered, he struggled out of the sludge torrent and flopped exhausted against the tunnel wall.

This was the darkest place he'd ever been in. For some reason his squiz molecules weren't working properly.

Perhaps, thought Wilton, my squiz molecules were stunned by the fall. Perhaps now they think they're taste molecules.

He did have a very strong taste of sludge in his food tube.

Wilton ignored it. He had something much more important to think about.

Meeting worms.

'Hello,' he called as he wriggled along the tunnel wall in the darkness. 'Is anyone here?'

He paused and listened. He knew his noise molecules were working because he could hear the sludge torrent thundering down in the distance behind him and the moaning of dazed enzymes as they slid slowly past him on what must be the sludge river.

But nothing else.

'Hello,' he called again. 'If you're a worm, I'd very much like to meet you. Or if you're a sludge god. Don't trouble yourself if you're a noodle.'

Nobody replied.

Wilton remembered how moody the sludge gods could be.

'Actually,' called Wilton, wriggling nervously on into the darkness, 'if you're a sludge god and you're busy, don't stop what you're doing for me. It's worms I really want to meet.'

Silence.

Wilton wriggled on.

'Hello,' he called. 'Newly arrived worm here hoping to meet long-lost family members.'

Not a single voice replied.

Wilton kept on hoping.

When you were in a scary dark sludge tunnel a long way from home, it was all you could do.

'This is hopeless,' said Wilton.

He rolled over onto his back. He'd been wriggling along the tunnel so long his tummy was raw and he'd been calling out so much his chat molecules were aching.

And still he was alone in the darkness.

Wilton felt despairing about something else too. The memory of the microbe being blown away by the storm.

A real worm would probably have been able to protect the poor little dope, thought Wilton. Accept it, you're just an oversized microbe with too many fat molecules. One thing you're definitely not is a worm.

'Strewth,' said a voice in the darkness. 'Check this out, everyone, it's a worm.'

Wilton tried to see where the voice was coming from.

He couldn't. But he could feel a large number of tendrils and plasma strands tickling his tummy. And his squiz molecules.

'Bit dopey-looking,' said another voice. 'But it's definitely a worm.'

Then suddenly Wilton could see again.

The first thing he saw was a group of microbes on his squiz molecules wiping sludge off their tendrils. The second thing he saw was that the boat microbe wasn't among them.

'G'day,' said one of the microbes. 'That sludge build-up on your viewing area was pretty crook. I think we got most of it off.'

'Thank you,' said Wilton.

But he was finding it hard to concentrate on gratitude. Or on relief at being able to see again.

'When you say worm,' asked Wilton, 'you don't mean noodle?'

'No way,' said the microbe. 'What's a noodle?'

Wilton saw there wasn't a single noodle in the sludge river flowing along the tunnel. They must have all been pulped at the bottom of the drop. When these microbes said worm, they meant worm.

Wilton felt excitement molecules fizzing inside him.

'I don't suppose there are any other worms around here?' he asked.

The microbes all shook their ectoplasms.

'There were once,' said another microbe. 'Yonks ago. Our myths and legends reckon worms used to visit this part of the intestine heaps.'

'This part of the what?' said Wilton.

The microbes pointed at the sludge tunnel.

'Intestine,' they said. 'It's just another name for the world.'

Wilton decided not to get into a discussion about how the world was a bit bigger than the microbes thought. Not now he'd realised that if he continued travelling along the intestine, chances were he'd probably meet some worms.

He turned to go. Then he remembered his manners.

'Thanks very much for helping me squiz again,' he said to the microbes. 'If there's ever anything I can do to repay the favour ...'

He realised the microbes weren't looking at him. They were peering anxiously along the intestine.

'Actually, there is,' said one of the microbes, turning back to him. 'Over here.'

The microbes all rushed over to where, Wilton saw, an acid spill covered the intestine wall.

'You turned up just in time,' said the microbes. 'We can't get across.'

Wilton saw the problem. Slowly moving sludge filled the rest of the intestine. Wilton knew some microbes were allergic to sludge. It gave them tendril rash and sore ectoplasms. And most microbes had an even worse reaction to acid. It made them shrivel up and melt. From all the frantic tendril waving going on now, he guessed this lot were shrivellers and melters.

'No problem,' said Wilton. 'I'll make a bridge.'

As he wriggled into the puddle, a thought

hit him. He'd often wondered why, unlike most microbes, his skin was acid-proof. Now he knew.

It's because I'm a worm.

Wilton lay across the acid puddle, glowing with happiness as well as the tingle of the acid on his skin. Luckily he was just long enough.

'Thanks, fatso,' yelled the microbes as they scampered across his back.

Wilton was curious. He'd never seen microbes in such a wild rush.

'What's the hurry?' he said.

'Behind you,' said the last of the microbes as it disappeared down the tunnel.

Wilton peered back along the length of his body. What he saw made him go so rigid with fear his whole body went into cramp.

Fungus.

Not the individual specks of floating fungus he was familiar with at home.

An evil boiling writhing cascade of furiously multiplying fungus spores advancing towards him along the intestine wall.

Wilton had never actually seen the horror of it close up, but he'd heard the terrifying legends the slime patch liked to tell.

And now it was almost on him.

Killer fungus.

Wilton tried desperately to stop being a bridge.

He couldn't.

He wanted to curl up in the middle of the acid puddle, safe from the frenzied mob advancing along the intestine wall. They wouldn't be able to get him when he was surrounded by acid. Wilton was pretty sure fungus wasn't acid-proof, even killer fungus.

But the cramp spasms were keeping him rigid.

He couldn't move.

The tip of his tail was poking out beyond the edge of the acid. The millions of specks of pure evil had almost reached it and Wilton could see they only had one thing on their mind.

Killing.

This is tragic, thought Wilton. Just when I've finally discovered I'm a worm, I'm going to be a dead worm.

He tried not to think about all the other worms he could have met. And made friends with. And had fun doing worm things with.

He wondered whether, if he explained he was on a mission to find a friend, the killer fungus would take pity on him.

Just this once.

Probably not.

Plus, he saw glancing back, it was too late. The first fungus spores were on his tail. He gritted his food tube and waited for the end.

Pain, the slime patch had reckoned.

Incredible pain.

'Arghhh,' giggled Wilton. 'Stop it. That tickles.'

It wasn't pain, it was very intense tickling.

Wilton's whole body writhed and twisted.

'Please,' he giggled. ' Stop. I can't bear it.'

His tail was writhing and twisting too, whacking into the acid puddle again and again.

'Hey, fatso,' yelled the fungus spores indignantly as they started to shrivel. 'Go easy on the whacking.'

The tickling was excruciating. Wilton couldn't have controlled his tail if he'd wanted to. The specks of fungus were flung off into the acid, swearing loudly as they melted.

The tickling stopped.

Weak with relief, the spasms gone, Wilton pulled his tail towards him and curled into a tight ball in the middle of the acid. The fungus army, seething with fury, started to surround the puddle.

'Won't do you any good,' muttered Wilton. 'You won't get me now, you vicious little mongrels.'

He felt like giving a gloating laugh. He didn't, partly because his laugh molecules were still a bit cramped, but mostly because he saw that the fungus was mounting an attack from above.

Oh no.

He'd forgotten that fungus spores could fly. Quite a few of them were doing it now, floating high over the acid puddle.

Wilton rolled in the acid, trying to cover his whole body with the stuff. But he knew it probably wouldn't work. If he missed one little patch, the floating fungus would zero in and he'd be history.

'The gland,' said a muffled voice. 'Wriggle into the gland.'

Wilton was startled. Where had that voice come from? Then he realised. It must be his think molecules frantically trying to find a way to escape.

Funny, he thought. They've never spoken to me like that before.

Above Wilton the mighty walls of the intestine curved upwards as high as he could see. He peered at them, looking for a gland.

He wished he knew what one looked like.

Then he saw, not too far up the wall, a small opening. Acid was dribbling out of it and down into the puddle.

'Don't just lie there,' said the voice. 'Get a wriggle on.'

The voice wasn't muffled this time. Wilton saw

why. Standing on his shoulder, waving its tendrils frantically, trying desperately to keep its feet on a dry patch, was the tiny microbe he'd last seen under the egg boat.

'Go,' said the microbe, waving wildly towards the gland.

Wilton didn't stop to ask questions.

The fungus hadn't quite surrounded the puddle. Wilton wriggled faster than he ever had before, through the rapidly shrinking gap in the fungus and towards the entrance to the gland.

As he powered up the intestine wall, Wilton glanced again at the microbe on his back. The little maniac was swatting at the descending fungus spores with what looked to Wilton like a jagged piece of the egg boat.

'What happened to your boat?' asked Wilton.

'Don't talk, Wriggles,' said the microbe. 'Just get into that gland.'

Wilton tried to get into the gland.

He wouldn't fit.

He tried again, ramming his shoulders against the narrow entrance.

It was no good.

'I'm too fat,' said Wilton miserably. 'Too fat and blubbery. You go. I'll squash as many spores as I can before they tickle me to death.'

'You're not too fat,' panted the microbe, still swatting. 'You're too tense and your molecules are all bunched up. Think of something relaxing.'

'I can't,' said Wilton.

'You can,' said the microbe. 'What relaxes you?'

'Gazing at sludge paddocks,' said Wilton. 'Sludge paddocks covered with enzymes getting lots of exercise so their drumsticks are low-fat.'

'Good,' said the microbe. 'What else?'

'I like to watch white blood cells rounding up viruses,' said Wilton. 'I love the delicate patterns the flocks of viruses make as they try to scamper away.'

'See?' said the microbe. 'It's working.'

You're right, thought Wilton. I am feeling more relaxed.

Wilton could feel his outer molecules getting less tense. As they relaxed, his body was feeling longer. And thinner.

'Get in there,' said the microbe.

Wilton wriggled into the gland. It was still a tight fit, but he was able to slither forward without too much difficulty. The slippery acid oozing out of the gland walls helped.

That microbe is a genius, thought Wilton once he was snugly inside. No way can the fungus get me in here.

Wilton sent some squiz molecules and chat molecules down to his rear end. The squiz molecules were to make sure the acid had covered the small part of his tail still visible to the fungus. The chat molecules were to send the fungus a message.

'Tough luck, you mongrels. Try and squeeze in here and you'll get fried.'

Then Wilton had a horrible thought.

The microbe probably didn't have acid-proof skin either. Was it getting fried too?

'Are you OK?' Wilton asked anxiously.

No answer. The microbe wasn't on his shoulder. Wilton didn't know where it was. He hoped it wasn't out in the intestine, trying to swat as many spores as it could before they tickled it to death.

Relax, Wilton said to himself. Anyone that brave and smart and well-organised knows how to look after itself.

He tried to feel convinced.

Then he remembered how easily the microbe had been blown off the cliff.

Suddenly Wilton couldn't stand the thought of one tiny microbe trying to hold off millions of killer fungus spores with a piece of broken eggshell. He wriggled backwards out of the gland, hoping his anxiety wouldn't make his molecules bunch up again.

He flopped out into the intestine, ready to fight.

The fungus had gone.

He couldn't see the microbe either.

'Hello,' said Wilton. 'Anyone here?'

No reply.

There was something eerie and lonely and sad about the vastness of the intestine. The huge tunnel was silent except for the soft squelch of moving sludge and the squeak of listless enzymes.

Wilton felt empty and listless himself as he

rubbed against the intestine wall to get the acid off his skin.

That little microbe was the first friend he'd ever had.

Perhaps the only friend.

'Hey, Wriggles,' said a voice. 'Why the long food tube? We made it.'

Wilton turned round.

The little microbe was standing behind him, tendrils out wide.

Wilton was so delighted he forgot to ask the microbe how it had survived in the acid gland.

'Actually,' said Wilton, 'my name's Wilton.'

'G'day,' said the microbe. 'I'm Algy.'

'Thank you, Algy,' said Wilton. 'You saved my life.'

'That might only be temporary,' said the microbe, clambering onto Wilton's shoulder. 'We'll probably run into more fungus on our journey, so we'd better keep a squiz out.'

Wilton wriggled round a bend in the intestine and felt Algy stiffen on his shoulder.

'Over there,' hissed Algy, waving his tendrils. 'A whole bunch of them.'

'Where?' said Wilton, peering at the spongy caves and slimy crevices that covered the walls of the intestine. The thought of finally meeting other worms made his food tube tingle with excitement.

'Do they look friendly?' he said, still trying to see them.

Algy didn't answer. Wilton realised that was because the little microbe had disappeared.

The worms seemed to have disappeared too. Wilton twisted around in circles but he couldn't see them anywhere.

Finally Algy reappeared on his shoulder.

'Sorry,' said Algy. 'False alarm. From a distance bits of dead microbe can look very like killer fungus spores.'

Wilton saw where Algy was pointing. Inside a cave were piles of microbe body parts. The tragic remains, Wilton guessed, of an old killer fungus raiding party.

Poor things, thought Wilton. And poor Algy, having to see other microbes in bits like that.

'I'm sorry too, Algy,' he said as they set off along the intestine again. 'I was looking for worms and forgetting to keep a squiz out for killer fungus.'

Algy patted him on the shoulder.

'Don't feel bad, Wriggles,' said Algy. 'I understand how much you want to meet your lot. But the whole world's in a mess. We're up to our tendrils in sick sludge and killer fungus and wild storms and headache epidemics. We've got to find out what's causing all this bad stuff.'

Wilton wanted to suggest that as there were two of them, perhaps they could do both things at once.

Meet worms and save the world.

He didn't.

Algy obviously felt very strongly about this.

Wilton knew friends were meant to support each other as much as possible, and even though being a friend was a very new experience for him, he wanted to do it right.

'OK,' he said.

'Good on you, Wilton,' said Algy. 'You're the biggest and strongest friend I've got. I need you.'

Wilton glowed.

This felt much better than being called fat and useless.

It was a long journey down the intestine, but Wilton didn't mind. Having a friend on his shoulder made all the difference.

They kept a careful squiz out for killer fungus and made a plan to save the world.

'If we keep following the enchanted circle of sludge,' said Algy, 'we're bound to find the problem sooner or later.'

'I agree,' said Wilton.

He didn't say 'and we'll probably meet some worms too' but he thought it.

'Wilton,' said Algy.

'Yes,' said Wilton guiltily, wondering if Algy could read his thoughts.

'You know before,' said Algy, 'when I was talking about us being up to our tendrils in bad stuff? Sorry, I didn't think when I said that. About you not having, you know, tendrils.'

'That's OK,' said Wilton.

Who needs tendrils, he thought happily, when you've got the bravest and most considerate friend in the world?

'I'm feeling very good about this journey,' said Algy. 'I think the worst is over. I reckon we've seen the last of those killer fungus mongrels, trust me.'

'I do,' said Wilton.

They wriggled round a bend in the intestine and found themselves in a vast cavernous space.

Full of killer fungus.

'Slithering sludge,' squeaked Algy.

Wilton was too terrified to say anything. The boiling seething fungus hordes were all around them. There was no escape. Wilton braced himself for agonising death-inducing pain. Or at least agonising death-inducing tickling.

But neither happened.

Wilton couldn't believe it.

The fungus spores didn't swarm all over him. The nearest ones just glanced at him and then carried on with what they were doing.

Fighting a huge battle.

Across the surface of a vast sludge plain, armies of fungus were hurling themselves against armies of tiny but determined defenders. White blood cells, Wilton saw. The elite troops of the immune system.

Except, Wilton noticed anxiously, they didn't look very elite at the moment. They were holding the fungus hordes off, but only just. The carnage was terrible. The dead on both sides were piling up faster than their enemies could eat them.

And still none of the fungus hordes were attacking Wilton.

'This is amazing,' he said to Algy. 'The mongrels mustn't be game to tangle with us now they know that tickling turns my tail into a ruthless killing machine.'

He looked at his shoulder to see if Algy agreed.

Algy wasn't there.

Wilton squizzed around, concerned. He couldn't see Algy anywhere. Then he noticed, at the far end of the sludge plain, the entrance to another tunnel.

I bet Algy's headed down there, thought Wilton. Leading me away from all this unpleasant killing.

He wriggled down to the new tunnel as fast as he could, taking care not to squash any of the dead bodies.

As soon as Wilton was in the tunnel, Algy appeared on his shoulder.

'Good on you, Wriggles,' he said. 'You read my mind.'

Wilton felt like having a word with Algy about running off like that, but there were more important things to talk about. He peered out at the battle raging across the sludge plain.

'Those white blood cells need help,' he said. 'I wish there was some way we could lend a tendril. Or in my case a tail.'

'Wilton,' said Algy. 'There are two of us. How many fungus spores are there?'

Wilton didn't bother trying to work it out. He'd never learned to count past a billion.

'I want to keep you in one piece, Wriggles,' said Algy. 'So please, don't get cocky with killer fungus. Come on, the best way we can help is to find out what's causing the fungus invasion in the first place.'

Wilton nodded, tingling inside.

He'd never had a friend who wanted to keep him in one piece before.

They headed along the tunnel.

After a while, Wilton noticed something strange about the sludge. It was hardly flowing at all here. He stopped and gave it a prod with his front molecules. It was almost solid.

'Algy,' he said. 'Look at this.'

'I know,' said Algy. 'Not good.'

A couple of fungus spores drifted past on their way to the battle. They ignored Wilton. Wilton, remembering Algy's advice, ignored them too.

'What do you think's making the sludge go like this?' he said to Algy.

Algy didn't reply.

Wilton saw he'd disappeared again.

How does he do that? thought Wilton, bewildered. I've seen microbes move fast when farmers get angry, but never that fast.

'Algy,' called Wilton as he hurried on down the tunnel. 'Are you OK?'

No Algy.

Not so much as a tendril.

Wilton wriggled round a bend, concern turning into panic, and stopped.

A huge drift of solid sludge was completely blocking the tunnel.

'Aha,' said Algy, appearing on Wilton's shoulder. 'This might be the problem we're looking for. But we won't know till we see what's on the other side.'

Wilton wanted to have a very stern word with Algy, but this didn't seem like the time. Instead he squizzed uncertainly at the wall of sludge. It did look very solid.

'I might be able to get us through,' he said.

'Give up, fatso,' said a cranky-looking amoeba lounging nearby. 'No way you'll get your blubber through that.'

'Don't listen to the miserable cell-sack,' said Algy to Wilton. 'If you wriggle hard enough you'll get through, I know you will.'

Wilton saw that Algy's ectoplasm was glowing with conviction and all his tendrils were clasped together fervently.

So this is what it feels like to have a friend who believes in you, thought Wilton.

It felt good, even if the friend did come and go a bit.

Wilton pressed his front molecules against the sludge drift and remembered how powerfully he'd wriggled when he was doing his exercises and had put his mind to it.

He put his mind to it now.

He started to bore into the hard sludge.

'Yes,' yelled Algy. 'You're doing it.'

Wilton wriggled so hard his food tube bulged out at the back.

'Now that,' said the amoeba, 'is a revolting sight.'

Slowly, painfully, but without stopping once to

eat the amoeba, Wilton tunnelled his way into the sludge.

After what felt like an age he had to have a rest. He wriggled back out and flopped down exhausted next to Algy.

'Brilliant,' said Algy. 'At this rate you'll be through in no time. What a champ.'

'Thanks,' said Wilton. 'I couldn't do it without you.'

'Aw,' crowed the amoeba. 'Isn't that sweet. The worm's thanking the germ.'

'That germ,' said Wilton sternly to the amoeba, 'happens to be my best friend.'

Algy glowed with pleasure, which made Wilton feel pretty good too.

But there was a job to be done.

'Better get back to it,' said Wilton, wriggling towards the sludge wall.

'Only when you feel ready, Wriggles,' said Algy. 'I know how exhausting it can be, trying to get through a difficult blockage. I've been in a similar situation myself inside your food tube.'

Wilton stopped. He wasn't sure he'd heard right. Perhaps his noise molecules had been damaged by all the tunnelling.

'Inside my food tube?' he said to Algy.

'That's right,' said Algy. 'Your food tube gets a bit jammed at times with all those low-fat enzyme drumsticks. Sometimes I've been stuck in there for ages.'

Wilton couldn't believe what he was hearing.

'You?' he whispered, horrified. 'Inside my food tube? You're joking, right?'

'No,' said Algy, looking puzzled.

'Hee hee hee,' chortled the amoeba. 'This is hilarious. Wriggles' best friend is a parasite who lives inside him and eats his guts.'

Wilton stared at Algy, weak with shock.

For a few dazed and disbelieving moments Wilton's think molecules felt as clogged and jammed as the sludge blocking the tunnel.

Then he managed to get some words out.

'Is that true?' said Wilton to Algy. 'Do you live inside me and eat my guts?'

Algy looked indignant, his tendrils all shrugging at once.

'No,' he said. 'I don't *live* inside you. I spend a fair bit of time inside you, but I don't *live* there.'

Wilton couldn't believe what he was hearing.

'And what about my guts?' he demanded, feeling sick. 'Do you eat them?'

Algy shrugged again, his tendrils flapping nervously.

'I don't *eat* them,' he said. 'I just sort of nibble on them sometimes when I'm hungry, but I don't, you know, *eat* them.'

Wilton stared at the tiny microbe, appalled.

He wished he was on a high ledge so he could fling himself off and roll down into a valley and get as far away from this monster as possible. But he couldn't. In front of him the tunnel was completely blocked with solid sludge. Behind him Wilton could hear the distant sound of killer fungus slaughtering white blood cells. He had no choice but to stay close to the revolting microbe who used to be his friend.

'Don't look like that,' said Algy. 'It's what I do. I'm a parasite. I use you for shelter and food, but that doesn't mean we can't be friends.'

Wilton was speechless.

'A parasite for a friend,' hooted the amoeba lounging nearby. 'Some dopes'll do anything to lose weight.'

Wilton gave the amoeba a long hard look.

The amoeba slithered away.

Wilton turned back to Algy.

'I see it all now,' said Wilton. 'You didn't really care about giving me my egg back, did you? You just wanted to get inside me and start noshing.'

Algy looked hurt.

'It wasn't like that,' he said. 'I wanted to help. But I also needed help. So I hopped on board the biggest and strongest individual in the valley.'

'The biggest and meatiest individual, you mean,' retorted Wilton. 'The one who'll give you the most meals until he finally drops dead, a gobbled-out husk.'

Algy waved his tendrils, exasperated.

'Use your think molecules, Wriggles,' he said. 'Why would I want to eat you to death when I need you to help me save the world?'

Wilton wanted to tell Algy to go and eat his own ectoplasm. He wanted to tell him to go and fry in an acid gland. But something in Algy's voice made Wilton feel suddenly uncertain.

What if Algy was telling the truth?

'I mostly just eat some of the food in your food tube,' said Algy. 'But when there's none there and I'm starving, I nibble your guts a bit. I'm sorry. They grow back, honest. If they didn't, I wouldn't touch them. I don't want to hurt you, Wriggles. I've been keeping you safe.'

'My name's Wilton,' said Wilton coldly.

'Sorry,' said Algy.

'How have you been keeping me safe?' said Wilton.

'Remember the tickling?' said Algy. 'When you were being a bridge over the acid puddle?'

Wilton remembered. If it hadn't been for the tickling, right now he'd be a fungus-riddled corpse.

'That was me,' said Algy. 'Tickling you from the inside.'

Wilton stared at him for a long time.

'How do you do it?' he said finally. 'Get in and out without me feeling anything?'

'Parasite training,' said Algy. 'I'll show you. Don't turn round.'

Wilton realised Algy was heading towards his rear end. Before he could stop him, he heard Algy's muffled voice.

'There, that didn't hurt, did it?'

Slithering sludge, thought Wilton. He's inside my tummy.

'I'm coming out,' called Algy.

Before Wilton could start a discussion about which exit Algy would use, he felt Algy scampering along his back. On the outside.

'In and out, don't make them shout,' said Algy, appearing on Wilton's shoulder. 'That's our motto.'

'Incredible,' muttered Wilton.

He hadn't felt a thing.

'Shall we get out of here?' said Algy. 'We're not going to save the world stuck in a sludge jam. And when those fungus hordes get through obliterating those poor blood cells, I reckon they'll be looking for more microbes to mangle.'

Wilton turned towards the hole he'd started in the sludge drift. There was a lot of tunnelling to be done.

'Just before you start again,' said Algy. 'I'm thinking you're going to need all your energy molecules to get through there, and I can help you with that, organising them and stuff, but I'll have to pop inside for a bit.'

'OK,' said Wilton.

He still wasn't crazy about the idea, but if it would help save the world and help him meet some worms he wasn't going to bicker about it.

Then an unpleasant thought hit him.

'When you go in and out,' he said to Algy, 'do you always use the . . .?'

'We always try to consider our hosts' feelings,' said Algy. 'Wherever possible we use the rear exit.'

Wilton wasn't sure if that was good news or not.

'Let's get a wriggle on,' said Algy.

'Do you feel hungry?' asked Wilton.

'Not at the moment,' said Algy.

'Good,' said Wilton.

Wilton wriggled and tunnelled and tunnelled and wriggled until he thought his front molecules were going to burst and his tail was going to fall off.

From time to time Algy's muffled voice encouraged him.

'Go, Wriggles.'

It helped, but the sludge drift was very thick. One by one, Wilton's energy molecules were burned up.

'It's no good,' wheezed Wilton. 'I can't go on.'

'You can,' said Algy's muffled voice. 'You have to. Here, I've found some more energy molecules. Oh no, sorry, they're part of your guts.'

Wilton was about to tell Algy to come out and lend a tendril when suddenly, with a last wriggling spasm, he burst through the sludge.

The first thing he realised about the tunnel on the other side was that it was very bright.

Brighter than anything he'd ever seen.

And that was before he'd wriggled out of the hole, dropped to the floor of the tunnel, curled up and wiped the sludge off his squiz molecules with his tail.

Then the tunnel was so bright he thought his squiz molecules were going to explode.

After quite a long time, when his squiz molecules had adjusted, Wilton realised something else about this end of the tunnel.

No sludge.

The tunnel curved away ahead of him, completely empty.

Amazing, thought Wilton.

He waited for Algy to reappear.

Algy didn't.

Probably feeling a bit embarrassed, thought Wilton. Now I know his guilty secret.

'Are you OK?' he called.

'Fine thanks,' replied Algy's muffled voice.

'Are you eating?' said Wilton suspiciously.

'No,' said Algy's voice guiltily.

You'd better not be, thought Wilton.

'Just doing a few repairs,' said Algy's voice.

Wilton felt faint.

'What do you mean?' he squeaked.

'Nothing serious,' said Algy's voice. 'Just a few internal stress fractures. From all the tunnelling.'

Wilton felt even fainter.

'I'll be out shortly,' said Algy's voice.

Wilton decided to explore.

Best if I keep occupied, he thought. Keep my mind off what that clown's doing in there.

He wriggled a little way along the tunnel.

And stopped.

In the tunnel wall was another gland, oozing a thick liquid. Wilton knew as soon as he saw it that it wasn't acid. It was sugar juice. He hadn't tasted sugar juice for ages. Sugar juice was banned for a fat microbe on a diet.

But, thought Wilton, I'm not a fat microbe any more. And I've got to eat for two now.

He started sucking in the delicious sugar juice.

'Yum,' yelled Algy's muffled voice. 'Don't stop.'

Wilton didn't stop until he felt completely full and Algy was beginning to complain about the risk of drowning.

Then Wilton headed on again.

While he explored, he thought about the solid sludge. The blockage meant that the enchanted circle of sludge was broken. Could this be the cause of all the world's problems? Was that how to save the world, unblock the sludge?

Better discuss it with Algy, thought Wilton.

But not just yet.

He decided to go a little further along the tunnel. Just in case this was where the worms lived, down here beyond the sludge. The world could wait a little bit longer to be saved.

Wilton hurried along the tunnel.

Right to the end.

Then he stopped and stared, gobsmacked.

'Algy, quick,' called Wilton, struggling to get the words out.

He wanted to turn and wriggle away. He wanted to go back to the known world where things were familiar and you could mostly understand them. But his molecules were frozen with terror and amazement and they wouldn't move.

'Algy,' whispered Wilton. 'I think you should see this.'

Wilton's squiz molecules had never known such searing whiteness. Not even the time a herd of albino enzymes had stampeded and flashed their bottoms at him.

'Ow,' said Algy, appearing on Wilton's shoulder and squinting. 'That's bright. Is that albino enzymes?'

'I don't think so,' said Wilton, squinting even harder.

He moved cautiously forward a few wriggles.

'I think it's the end of the sludge tunnel,' he said.

'That's impossible,' said Algy. 'The tunnel can't just end. What about the enchanted circle of sludge? If the tunnel just ends, how does the sludge flow back to our valley?'

Wilton didn't know.

All he knew was that they'd just wriggled out the end of the tunnel and they were now in a valley that was so big it made their valley at home look like a wrinkle.

'Look at those two huge round hills,' squeaked Algy. 'They're . . . they're . . . huge.'

Wilton was already looking at them and was already amazed.

But that was nothing compared to what he felt when his squiz molecules started to get used to the brightness and he saw what was covering the two hills.

'Are those worms?' gasped Wilton.

They looked like worms, white just like him, but much longer.

Much, much longer.

The curious thing was that the worms were woven together, like the matted whiskers and dead plasma strands in the old farmer's coat at home.

There were thousands of them.

Wilton gazed up, awestruck.

This must be how worms hang out together, he said to himself. When there's more than one of them.

More than one of us.

The thought made Wilton's molecules buzz with joy and dizzy excitement.

Algy was staring up at the woven worms too.

'Um,' he squeaked, 'I think I'll leave the g'days to you, Wriggles.'

Algy vanished. His muffled voice came from inside Wilton's food tube.

'If you need me, I'm in here.'

'Algy,' said Wilton. 'There's no need to be scared. They won't hurt you, they're worms.'

Algy didn't reply.

Microbes, thought Wilton, exasperated. Since I stopped being one, I understand them less and less.

Trembling with anticipation, Wilton wriggled up the hill to meet the worms.

'Hello,' he said when he got closer.

The worms didn't reply.

'I'm a worm too,' said Wilton, in case the woven worms hadn't noticed.

He couldn't tell if they had or not, because they still didn't reply.

Perhaps they haven't got noise molecules, thought Wilton.

There was a type of amoeba in the valley at home that didn't have noise molecules. They were always falling off ledges, even when you yelled a warning at them. Though that was partly because they didn't have squiz molecules either.

Wilton wriggled from side to side, hoping the woven worms did at least have squiz molecules and could see he was waving at them.

Nope.

They weren't waving back.

'You're completely wasting your time,' said a nearby voice.

For a moment Wilton thought Algy had come out to help, but then he saw a couple of protozoa on the hillside, peering down their tendrils at him and shaking their scorn molecules.

'Should I go further up the hill?' said Wilton. 'Get closer?'

'It's not a hill, you absurd creature,' said one of the protozoa. 'It's a buttock.'

'A buttock?' said Wilton, puzzled.

'You're completely wasting your time,' said the protozoa, 'with all that ridiculous waving.'

'Why?' said Wilton. 'Are those worms squiz-impaired as well as noise-impaired?'

'They're not worms, foolish boy,' said the other protozoa. 'They're underpants.'

'Underpants?' said Wilton.

He didn't have a clue what the protozoa were on about.

'You won't get a conversation going with underpants,' said the first protozoa. 'I've never heard a squeak out of underpants.'

'Socially,' said the other protozoa, 'underpants are very boring.'

Wilton was very confused. Were underpants a species that went about disguising themselves as worms so they'd be more popular at parties? Or were they huge transparent creatures who just ate a lot of worms?

Wilton feared that might be it.

The poor matted worms hadn't moved at all.

Backing away from the underpants, Wilton decided to ask the protozoa for a bit more information. But before he could, the protozoa both started shrieking and waving their plasma strands and running off.

Oh no, thought Wilton, glancing fearfully upwards. The underpants must be hungry again.

He needn't have worried.

The underpants weren't doing anything aggressive. Just moving and stretching a bit.

Perhaps I'm wrong, thought Wilton hopefully. Perhaps underpant is simply the name of a type of worm that likes to cuddle other worms in a neat and orderly sort of way.

It was possible.

Then Wilton saw what was causing the underpants to move and stretch. What was terrifying the protozoa.

'Arghhh,' he screamed.

More worms.

Completely different ones.

Five huge pink worms, side by side, hurtling towards him. Gliding between the underpants and the hills.

They were so massive that Wilton couldn't move at first. Just gape in stunned terror at their pink hugeness and their gargantuan armoured hoods.

Then he turned and wriggled for his life.

But the massive worms were too fast.

Wilton felt their vast shadows fall over him. He curled himself up tight, hoping somehow he could escape being squashed or crushed or pulverised.

The giant worms thudded into the hillside just past Wilton. For a fleeting moment he thought they hadn't seen him. But then, balancing grotesquely on their armoured hoods, all five of them started scraping backwards towards him, making huge indentations in the hillside as they went.

'Algy,' screamed Wilton. 'Run.'

'Soon as I can,' replied Algy's muffled voice. 'I'm, er, just finishing a few things in here.'

Before Wilton could repeat his warning, one of the giant worms smashed into him. For a sickening instant, Wilton thought he was dead. Then he realised he was jammed in a cavity between the tip of the worm and its armoured hood.

The cavity was about the size of the neighbours' cave back home.

Wilton struggled not to think of home and how he'd probably never see it again.

'Algy,' he screamed. 'Get out. Run for it.'

The worm was moving at incredible speed. From under the armoured hood, all Wilton could see was a blur of white underpants.

Algy appeared on his shoulder, looking terrified.

'What's happening?' he said.

'Worms,' said Wilton. 'We're on one.'

'They're not worms, you tiresome youth,' said a nearby voice.

Wilton peered around. Wedged between the wall of the cavity and his bottom were the two protozoa.

'They're fingers,' said one.

'Only four of them are, to be precise,' said the other. 'One's a thumb.'

'Yes, but we're on a finger,' said the first protozoa testily. 'Jammed under a fingernail.'

Wilton still didn't have a clue what the protozoa were on about.

Then everything went so bright it made the brightness of the underpants seem dull and grey.

Wilton couldn't see anything for what felt like ages. And when his squiz molecules finally started to make out some shapes, he thought he was dreaming.

The fingers were attached to the end of a humungous tendril. A tendril, Wilton calculated in a daze, big enough for about a billion farm workers to have their holidays on, including golf.

'That tendril is huge,' he croaked.

'It is not a tendril,' said one of the protozoa. 'It is an arm.'

Wilton barely heard.

Because there was more.

The tendril was attached to a body.

A body very different to any organism Wilton had ever seen. A body so big Wilton's think molecules went numb as he stared at it. A body that moved through space with the awesome majesty of an entire world.

'I don't get it,' squeaked Algy. 'What's going on?'

Wilton wasn't sure how to explain it himself.

It felt crazy even to think it.

But the truth was here, in front of his own squiz molecules.

The entire world, the world he'd grown up in, was alive.

'Slithering sludge,' squeaked Algy. 'The world's a very big microbe.'

It sounded crazy, but Wilton had to agree.

'We're on the end of one of its tendrils,' squeaked Algy. 'The world's alive and it's got fingernails.'

It still sounded crazy, but Wilton still had to agree.

Squiz molecules didn't lie.

Not even when they were gobsmacked with amazement.

The tendril was moving in great whooshing swoops and Wilton's insides were doing the same, but he could see that the world looming over him in all its vast hugeness did look like a kind of microbe. It had a main body section that was definitely microbe-shaped. It seemed to be going somewhere with huge lumbering strides. In a hurry like half the microbes Wilton had ever met.

There were a few differences though.

This microbe was several billion times larger than any microbe Wilton had ever seen. Plus it only had two tendrils for running around on and two for flapping instead of the usual eight or twelve.

And then there was the extra body section up top. None of the microbes Wilton knew had an extra body section like that. A round one with loads of curly dark plasma strands hanging out the top and holes in the front that blinked and sniffed and sobbed.

'Jeepers,' squeaked Algy. 'It's leaking.'

'I think it's upset about something,' said Wilton.

'Not us, I hope,' said Algy, retreating towards Wilton's rear entrance.

Wilton didn't think so. He was pretty sure the humungous microbe couldn't even see them, but for Algy's sake he tried to wriggle further under the protective shelter of the fingernail.

'Oi,' protested an irate voice behind him. 'Do you mind?'

Wilton remembered the two protozoa wedged behind his bottom. He wriggled forward as far as he could, which wasn't far because he didn't want to fall out from under the fingernail.

'Sorry,' he said.

But it wasn't the two protozoa who dragged themselves out, glaring at Wilton and pushing their ectoplasms back into shape. It was several hundred squashed and surly bacteria.

'Jiffing great fat lump,' grumbled one of the

bacteria. 'Jiff off. It's crowded enough under this fingernail without a flabby jiffing lardball like you barging in.'

'Yeah,' said another. 'Go find your own luxury accommodation, you big fat harpic.'

Wilton ignored them.

He saw that Algy, who had reappeared on his shoulder, wasn't going to be as restrained.

'Hey,' said Algy, waving his tendrils indignantly at the bacteria. 'We are witnessing one of the most incredible sights in the whole of microbe history. Do you think you could keep a lid on the bickering and insults just this once?'

The bacteria all stared at Algy as if he was several molecules short of a nucleus.

'What are you on about, handy andy?' they said. 'What incredible sight?'

Algy rolled his disbelief molecules and pointed to the vast heavenly body attached to their fingernail.

'The world,' he said. 'OK?'

The bacteria thought about this, crinkling their ectoplasms in puzzled frowns.

'That's not a jiffing world,' one of them said. 'That's our Janet.'

Wilton stared at the bacteria, wondering if he'd heard right.

'Your janet?' he said. 'What's a janet?'

'Surf and ajax,' said one of the bacteria. 'You're really dumb, aren't you?'

'Our janet's a giant living organism,' said another. 'Carbon based, metabolises oxygen, very intelligent, hates jiffing spinach.'

Wilton started to understand. He'd heard two wise old patches of slime arguing once about whether there was anything beyond the known world, and one of them had said something about 'outer space'. Another had used a word that Wilton was pretty sure was 'janets'.

He pointed to the huge janet they were orbiting.

'Does this mean we're in outer space?' he asked the bacteria.

He peered around. Outer space was very blue. Except for the lower part which was green. It looked to Wilton like a happy sort of place. He couldn't understand why a janet floating in it would be unhappy. There might even be worms in outer space.

The bacteria had crinkled their ectoplasms again.

'Where the domestos did you grow up?' said one to Wilton.

'This isn't outer space, toilet duck,' said another. 'It's the park next to the library. Pine-o-clean, what an idiot.'

Wilton started to ask what a park next to a library was, then changed his mind. There was something more important he needed to know.

'Why is the janet so upset?' he said. 'There's liquid coming out of her upper body section.'

'Oh, lah-de-dah,' said one of the bacteria. 'Upper body section.'

'Round here we call a face a jiffing face,' said another. 'She's crying. It's because the others are being mean to her.'

Others? thought Wilton. What others?

Then his squiz molecules almost fell out of his ectoplasm with amazement. In the distance, coming into view, were several other huge janets.

'Rough kids from down the street,' said one of the bacteria. 'They're right little napisans.'

Wilton was totally confused. He could see Algy was too.

'They're chasing our Janet,' said another of the bacteria. 'She's running away from them. Well, trying to, she's a bit slow. If they catch her, we'll all be in the palmolive. When she cries for a long time she rubs her eyes and those salty tears sting like draino.'

Wilton's anxiety molecules trembled inside him.

The other janets were getting closer.

Algy headed for cover.

Suddenly it was all too much for Wilton as well. Ever since they'd left the sludge tunnel, everything had been almost too amazing to take in. And too confusing. And too scary.

Wilton headed for cover like Algy. He apologised to the bacteria and wriggled as far under the fingernail as he could. He was feeling so weak and shaky he was worried about slipping in a puddle of bacteria dribble and skidding off into outer space or outer library park or whatever the jiff it was called.

All I want, thought Wilton, is something to happen that I can recognise and understand.

Algy's plaintive muffled voice came from inside him. 'Why can't this janet go faster?'

'She's too fat,' said one of the bacteria.

'Way too fat,' said another.

'A real jiffing porker,' added a third. 'That's why all the others make fun of her.'

Wilton digested this.

He stopped feeling sorry for himself and stared at the other janets. They'd almost caught up. Wilton couldn't understand what they were yelling, but he could tell from the tone of their voices they were probably using words like 'fatso' and 'lardbucket'.

He looked up at his own janet. Her face was wet with unhappiness.

Poor thing, he thought. I'm only a worm wedged under a fingernail and you're a mighty janet, but I know how you feel.

Then one of the bacteria started groaning and hugging itself.

'Blu loo,' it moaned through its tendrils. 'It's happening again. Our Janet's too stressed. I'm getting a colgate migraine.'

The other bacteria started doing the same, groaning and lying down.

Wilton stared at them.

He remembered the farm workers getting headaches at home. And the livestock. And the slime patches. The neighbours' cave had even had a migraine recently.

Suddenly Wilton started to understand.

11

'Oh scotchguard,' groaned the bacteria, rubbing their ectoplasms with their tendrils. 'Our jiffing heads are splitting. Anyone got any aspirin molecules?'

Wilton felt sorry for them, but not as sorry as he did for the sobbing janet who was carrying them through outer space under her fingernail.

He gazed up at the janet's huge unhappy face. Then he squizzed again at the other janets, which were orbiting closer and closer around her, jeering.

Her problem was much worse than a headache.

It was deeply tragic.

'Algy,' said Wilton to his tummy. 'I think I've worked out what's going on.'

Algy peeped out of Wilton's rear entrance, looking anxiously at the other janets.

'I've worked out what's going on too,' said Algy. 'We're trapped in the middle of an inter-janetary war.'

Wilton nodded towards the groaning bacteria.

'I think I've worked out what's causing all the problems at home,' he said. 'Stress.'

'Tell me about it,' said Algy. 'I'm getting a migraine myself.'

Wilton struggled to be patient. He reminded himself that he was a worm, not a microbe. Microbes could be excused for panicking because they were so much smaller. To them outer space must seem huge.

'When the other janets give our janet a hard time for being plump,' said Wilton, 'she gets upset and stressed. I know exactly how she feels.'

'I know you do,' said Algy, scampering onto Wilton's shoulder. 'When the bacteria called you a great fat lump just now, your food tube went into knots. I nearly got strangled.'

Wilton tried not to picture it.

'Exactly,' he said. 'So imagine how much stress a whole janet must feel. Bulk stress. Enough to cause widespread storms. And sick sludge. And fungus invasions.'

He could see that Algy was taking this in.

Wilton's think molecules were working overtime too.

'Listen,' he said to Algy. 'What if we could cheer our janet up? Make her less stressed. That might stop the problems at home getting worse. It might even improve things.'

Algy rolled his squiz molecules.

'Get real, Wriggles,' he said. 'We're a microbe and a worm. How can two little squirts like us cheer up a janet the size of her?'

Wilton thought hard.

'I know,' he said. 'We could meet some really interesting and funny worms and introduce her to them and get the worms to tell her jokes.'

Algy just looked at Wilton.

'OK,' said Wilton. 'There would be a small language problem. And she might not enjoy jokes about things crawling out of her bottom.'

'Here's what I think,' said Algy. 'We're the only ones on the whole janet who know what's causing the problems back home. We have to get back quick smart and tell the others.'

Wilton couldn't argue with that.

He wanted to. He wanted to say, 'no, I'm staying here in outer space to meet some worms'. But he didn't. Algy was right. They had to help the others at home if they could.

'I've been watching you,' said Algy, squiz molecules shining. 'Watching how brave you are. You don't run away from killer fungus or insults or underpants. I've decided to try and be more like you. So come on, let's go and warn the others.'

Wilton tried to. But his body wouldn't move. And it wasn't worm regrets that were stopping him.

'I'm stuck,' said Wilton.

His body was wedged tight under the fingernail.

77

'I must have wriggled in too far,' said Wilton.

Algy rolled his exasperation molecules.

'I'll see if I can get you unwedged from the inside,' he said, and disappeared.

While Algy rummaged around inside him, Wilton peered wistfully up at the janet and tried to think of another way of cheering her up. He decided he'd even consider something that didn't involve worms.

But what?

'Forget her,' grumbled one of the bacteria. 'How about cheering us up?'

Wilton looked at the groaning stress-afflicted slightly squashed bacteria.

'Have you tried telling each other jokes?' he suggested.

The bacteria looked unimpressed.

'Jiff off,' they said.

Before Wilton could tell them what he thought of their lack of gratitude, a pain stabbed through his middle.

'Ow,' said Wilton. 'That hurts.'

'Are we still wedged?' called Algy's muffled voice from inside Wilton's tummy. 'I'm seeing if I can dislodge us by moving a few things around in here.'

'We're still wedged,' said Wilton. 'And make sure you put everything back where you found it.'

To take his mind off what Algy might be doing, Wilton had another squiz up at the janet.

Poor thing, he thought.

She was still running and her fingernail and everyone under it were still jolting with each mighty step, so her sad face looked a bit blurred to Wilton's bouncing squiz molecules. But that made it easier for him to imagine what her face might look like if she was happy.

And what the valley at home might look like.

Storm-free with sparkling healthy sludge.

Suddenly Wilton had an idea to get him and Algy out from under the fingernail and started on their journey.

'Tickle me,' he yelled to Algy.

'Eh?' replied Algy's muffled voice.

'Like before,' said Wilton. 'Use anything lying around in there that's furry.'

Algy didn't reply, but soon Wilton felt the familiar tickling.

'No,' he giggled. 'More, more.'

The bacteria looked at him sourly.

'All right for some harpics,' said one of them. 'Good-time fatso worms and their party parasites.'

Wilton's whole body writhed and twisted with the excruciating tickling.

'Please,' he giggled. 'I can't bear it. Don't stop.'

He flung himself from side to side.

But it didn't work. He was still wedged tight.

'Sorry,' called Algy's muffled voice. 'It's a bit cluttered in here for tickling.'

Before Wilton could urge him to try harder,

nibbling some guts if necessary, the bacteria gave terrified yells.

'Colgate! Palmolive! Look out!'

Wilton peered around in alarm. And yelled himself.

Their janet was heading straight for a huge mass of tangled tendrils. Strange thick crooked brown ones with huge green platforms sprouting from them.

'It's a jiffing tree,' yelled one of the bacteria.

'Domestos,' screamed another. 'Watch out for the branches.'

'Watch out for the napisan leaves,' screeched a third.

Wilton saw that the janet was raising her fingers in front of her face. Including the finger he and Algy were on.

'We're going in,' screamed Wilton.

Something slapped him hard. Not the hysterical bacteria, something much bigger and greener.

For a few moments his squiz molecules were in chaos.

Then he saw he wasn't under the fingernail any more, he was on one of the huge green platforms the bacteria had called leaves.

He peered around, panicked. And saw the janet way over in the distance, not running now, just crouching and panting and rubbing her fingers.

Slithering sludge, thought Wilton. We're on another janet.

He looked up.

Towering above him was the biggest body he'd ever seen. It went so far up into outer space he couldn't see where it ended. Sprouting from it were masses of the huge crooked brown tendrils, swaying gently. Attached to them were millions of the green platforms.

Wilton started to wonder, dread molecules trembling, about what other creatures might live on this janet.

'Shall I stop tickling now?' called Algy's muffled voice.

'Yes,' whispered Wilton.

'Are we still under the fingernail?' asked Algy's voice.

'No,' whispered Wilton.

'Hooray,' yelled Algy's voice. 'That's great.'

'Not really,' said Wilton.

'Brilliant,' beamed Algy as he emerged from inside Wilton. 'Free from that sludge-forsaken fingernail at last. Now we can get back home and tell the others about ...'

He trailed off as he took in the large green leaf platform he and Wilton were perched on.

And the dark crooked branch tendrils all around them.

And the impossibly tall rough-skinned body towering above them.

'Slithering sludge,' squeaked Algy. 'Where are we?'

'On another janet,' said Wilton. 'I tried to tell you but you were cheering too loudly.'

'Is it a friendly janet?' whispered Algy.

'Don't know,' said Wilton.

He squizzed around anxiously for signs of aggressive locals. Killer fungus or heavily armed enzymes or giant amoeba that could suck your insides out through your rear exit.

He couldn't see any so far.

'Where's our janet?' asked Algy.

'Over there,' said Wilton, pointing with his tail.

Their janet was just visible in the distance, sitting on the ground with her head in her tendrils. Wilton was pleased to see that the other janets, the jeering ones, didn't seem to be around any more.

Algy was peering up again at the towering body above them.

'Wriggles,' he said. 'Do you think there's any chance this janet'll go over and say g'day to our janet so we can jump back on?'

'Not a hope,' said a deep voice.

Wilton spun round so fast Algy almost fell off his shoulder.

Approaching them across the leaf was a large yellow and orange striped worm.

Wilton wasn't sure whether to be delighted or scared.

He felt Algy hurrying towards his rear end. But instead of disappearing inside, Algy stopped and glared at the yellow and orange worm.

'That's a very negative attitude,' declared Algy.

Oh no, thought Wilton. Don't start being brave now, please.

The yellow and orange worm frowned and made a threatening move towards Algy.

'You looking for a fight?' it growled.

Algy disappeared inside. Then peeped out again.

'What makes you so sure?' he said. 'What makes you so sure this janet won't go visiting our janet, eh, stripey-bum?'

Wilton tried to yell at Algy, but his chat molecules had all fainted.

'I'll do you,' growled the yellow and orange worm, lunging at Algy.

Algy disappeared.

'You haven't answered my question,' called his muffled voice from inside Wilton.

'This is a tree,' growled the worm. 'Trees don't make social calls.'

'How do you know?' said Algy's muffled voice. 'They just might not tell you when they do.'

'They've got roots,' said the worm, glaring at Wilton's stomach and flexing its powerful-looking neck muscles. 'Roots are fixed. They don't move.'

'Well that just shows how much you know,' said Algy's muffled voice. 'Because this is outer space and everything moves in outer space, doesn't it, Wriggles?'

'Um,' said Wilton. 'I'm not really . . .'

Part of him wanted to back Algy up, but a bigger part of him wanted Algy to shut up.

'Just as well my best friend's a worm, lolly-features,' yelled Algy's muffled voice. 'Otherwise, meeting you, I'd be thinking all worms are idiots.'

'Algy,' squeaked Wilton to his tummy. 'Calm down.'

He turned back to the yellow and orange worm.

'Please forgive Algy,' he said. 'We've been under a lot of stress lately. He didn't mean to offend you.'

The yellow and orange worm didn't reply at first, just paused for a while, not moving. Then it flexed all its muscles.

'I'm not offended,' said the worm. 'Mostly because I'm not a worm, I'm a caterpillar.'

'Oh,' said Wilton.

Part of him was relieved and part of him was disappointed.

'Lucky for your friend I've been doing an anger management course,' added the caterpillar, nodding towards Wilton's stomach. 'Otherwise I'd take that cheeky little microbe apart molecule by molecule.'

'Is that right?' yelled Algy's muffled voice. 'Well why don't you come and get me then?'

'Algy,' said Wilton. 'Be quiet.'

He was relieved to see the caterpillar looking a tiny bit amused.

'Sorry,' said Wilton to the caterpillar.

'Internal parasites are all a bit mental,' said the caterpillar. 'They don't get out enough.'

Wilton's smile molecules were tingling. He liked this bloke.

'Are you sure you're not a worm?' he asked.

''Cause I'm a worm and I've been really hoping to meet some other worms.'

'Sorry, mate, can't help you,' said the caterpillar.

'We could be related,' said Wilton hopefully. 'I mean we both wriggle. And we're both very patient with dopey microbes. We could be distant cousins.'

The caterpillar wasn't looking even a tiny bit amused now.

'I don't think we are,' it said. 'I live on trees and eat leaves, you crawl out of the bottoms of fat mammals.'

'I suppose so,' said Wilton, disappointed. He wasn't sure what a mammal was, but he guessed it must be another name for a janet.

Suddenly he felt an indignant movement inside his tummy. It wasn't his molecules, it was Algy.

'Trees and leaves, eh?' yelled Algy's muffled voice. 'So you're a parasite too, veggie-bum.'

'We're all parasites,' said the caterpillar, glowering. 'Surely you know that?'

'Yes,' said Wilton hurriedly. 'Yes, we do.'

He didn't dwell on the thought for long, because the caterpillar was frowning again. It looked like it had decided to go in and get Algy after all. Either that or it was listening to something.

Wilton hoped it was the second of these. He could hear strange noises but he couldn't see where they were coming from.

'Look,' said the caterpillar, 'if you want to meet

some relatives, you'll find some on that bloke down there.'

Wilton peered down. And saw an amazing sight.

Jumping and panting and rolling and snuffling around the base of the tree was another janet. This janet was only a fraction of the size of Wilton's janet, and it was covered in thick dark curly plasma strands.

'It's called a dog,' said the caterpillar. 'Loads of your lot on that fella.'

Wilton stared down, fascinated.

The dog was frolicking as happily as an enzyme on healthy sludge.

'You could roll off here and drop down onto him easy as leaf pie,' said the caterpillar.

'I could,' said Wilton.

It was very tempting.

Wilton thought about what it would be like to meet real worms for the first time in his life. Other folk who looked like him and had the same thoughts and feelings and ticklish bits as him.

Then he remembered that he and Algy were meant to be getting back to their janet so they could tell everyone at home about the stress.

Wilton thought about what it would be like to go back home, where he'd still be the odd one out and where everyone would probably still call him fatso.

Maybe, he thought, we could put off going back home just for a little while.

'If you roll off my leaf pretty soon,' said the caterpillar, moving closer to Wilton and flexing his big muscles again, 'I won't have to pull your friend's insides out through your rear exit.'

'Good point,' said Wilton. 'Thanks.'

He rolled off the leaf.

Wilton had never fallen onto a dog before.

As he fell he hoped that the surface of the dog, with its covering of thick dark curly plasma strands, would be soft.

It wasn't.

Up close the plasma strands were almost as wide as Wilton. They were also coarse and rough. Wilton crashed through them and landed on the surface with an Algy-jarring thud.

'Ouch,' said Algy's muffled voice. 'What was that?'

'Nothing to worry about,' said Wilton to his tummy.

'Let me know if stripey-bum's pushing you around,' said Algy's muffled voice. 'Say the word and I'll be straight out to help. Just as soon as I've finished lunch.'

'I will,' replied Wilton. 'Thanks. I'm fine.'

He felt guilty about not being completely honest

with Algy, but he just didn't feel ready yet to break the news about them being on a dog.

Probably best if I explore a bit first, thought Wilton. Then, once I've got the lie of the land, I can show Algy around and he won't feel quite so shocked about being on a new janet. Particularly when I explain to him how close he came to being caterpillar sandwich spread.

Wilton headed off to look for worms.

It was hard going. The dog's plasma strands were a thick forest that covered its whole surface. They were so close together that Wilton had to struggle sometimes to wriggle between them.

And the dog never stopped moving. If it wasn't jumping or running, it was darting or lurching. One time it shook itself and Wilton had to wedge himself between a couple of plasma strands so he wouldn't be shaken off.

Phew, he thought when the shaking had stopped. Thank sludge I'm plump.

Then there were the microbes.

They were everywhere, clinging to the forest canopy and glaring down at Wilton.

'G'day,' said Wilton. 'Nice dog you've got here.'

'Woof,' said the microbes.

'I'm actually hoping to meet some worms,' said Wilton. 'I don't suppose you can point me in the right direction?'

'Woof,' said the microbes.

Wilton decided not to push it. Some of the

dog microbes had started growling and he had a feeling they wouldn't mind having a chew on his molecules.

'Everything OK out there?' called Algy's muffled voice. 'If veggie-bum's getting difficult, just say the word.'

'It's OK,' replied Wilton.

'I can tickle you if you need me to,' said Algy. 'You know, flip us off the leaf.'

'Thanks,' said Wilton, 'but I'm fine.'

As it turned out, the worms found Wilton.

He was just starting to wonder if he was going round in circles. The dog forest all looked the same and so did the dog microbes. Then he heard a slithering and a wriggling.

Wilton knew it wasn't him making the sound because he'd stopped wriggling to try and work out where exactly on the dog he was, and to try and pluck up the courage to break the news to Algy.

He turned round.

And saw, wriggling towards him through the forest, a group of worms.

Wilton's molecules buzzed with happiness and excitement.

The worms looked just like him. And, he saw with an extra surge of delight, they had squiz molecules and food tubes, so they weren't noodles.

'G'day,' said Wilton.

He waited, hope molecules frozen, to see if the

worms spoke like him too. Delighted as he was to see them, it would be a disappointment if all they could say was 'woof'.

'G'day,' said the worms, wagging their tails.

Wilton glowed.

'I'm Wilton,' he said.

'Wow,' said one of the worms. 'It's true. A visitor.'

'We love visitors,' said another worm. 'Though most of the ones we get around here are fleas.'

'Where are you from?' asked a third worm.

Wilton peered out through the forest. In the distance he could just make out his janet, still sitting sadly by herself.

'That janet over there,' he said.

The worms all looked.

'Poor kid,' said one. 'She looks like she needs cheering up.'

Wilton forced himself not to think about it. Not now, not while his dream was coming true at last.

'I'm so pleased to meet you,' he said to the worms. 'What's it like living here?'

'Great,' said one. 'We have heaps of fun. We visit drains and garbage bins and everywhere. This morning we were thrown out of a supermarket. We don't have an owner so we can do anything we want.'

Wilton didn't understand all the details, but the general picture sounded wonderful.

'Hey,' said one of the worms. 'Do you want to come and see our footy pitch? It wags.'

'I'd love to,' said Wilton happily.

Wilton's new friends showed him all over the dog, and Wilton was interested to see how similar it was to his janet, apart from the fur and the tail.

The worms showed Wilton how to wriggle out of the way when the dog licked its own bottom. Wilton was grateful, and amazed. He wondered if his own janet could do that.

The worms also showed him how to crawl out onto the dog's dangly bits and hang on for dear life when the dog shook itself. Once Wilton got used to the feeling of having his molecules scrambled, he enjoyed it.

But he did worry a bit about Algy, who hadn't said a word for ages.

He'll be fine, Wilton told himself. Probably just sleeping off a big lunch of my guts.

To take his mind off the guilt molecules prickling inside him, Wilton asked the worms if they'd show him around the dog's intestines.

'Best leave that till later,' said one of the worms. 'He's just had lunch out of a garbage bin and there might be some chunks of washing detergent floating around in there.'

Instead, while the dog had a sleep, the worms took Wilton back into the fur forest to ski down some flea bites. After lots of runs, they all sprawled out, happy and exhausted, for a doze themselves.

'We like you,' said one of the worms to Wilton.

Half-asleep, Wilton glowed happily.

'You can live here with us if you want,' said another worm.

Wilton wondered if he'd died and become a sludge god.

'So can your friend,' said a third worm.

That's strange, thought Wilton sleepily. How do they know about Algy?

'Slithering sludge,' squeaked a familiar voice.

Wilton snapped wide awake. Algy was on his shoulder, peering around in a state of shock.

He didn't look happy.

'Don't mind me,' said Algy. 'Don't let me interrupt you. I'm just getting my bearings in this new place, wherever it is.'

'Algy,' said Wilton. 'I'm sorry. I was planning to tell you just as soon as I . . .'

He didn't know what to say.

'Just as soon as you'd made some new friends,' said Algy. 'And some plans for the rest of your life that don't include me or the folks back home.'

'Algy . . .' said Wilton.

He could see how hurt Algy was.

'I'm fine,' said Algy, scrambling off Wilton's shoulder. 'Have a good time with your new friends. I can make new friends too.'

Algy headed over towards a pack of dog microbes.

'Hi there,' he said to the microbes. 'Can anyone tell me how to get out of this place?'

'Woof,' said the microbes.

Wilton watched him, feeling awful.

'He'll be OK,' said one of the worms. 'When he realises what a great place this is, he'll thank you for bringing him here.'

Wilton wasn't so sure.

Algy was surrounded by mean-looking dog microbes. They were sniffing him and growling at him and doing strange things to his lower tendrils.

'Stop that,' Algy was shouting. 'Back off. Sit.'

Wilton watched miserably. He wished Algy had the egg boat to hide under. He turned away, feeling even more jumbled inside than when Algy had rearranged his major organs.

He tried to think straight.

I'm not a microbe, I'm a worm. I belong here with the other worms. Algy's free to go back to where he belongs. I can't hold his tendril forever. He'll make it back on his own.

Probably.

Perhaps.

Wilton tried to think about something else. About all the good times he was going to have with the other worms for the rest of his life.

'Ow,' wailed Algy.

'Leave the visitor alone,' one of the worms yelled at the dog microbes. 'Bad microbes. I don't know what's got into you. You're behaving worse than fungus.'

Suddenly Wilton knew he couldn't do it.

He spoke up quickly, before he changed his mind.

'Thanks for inviting me to stay,' he said to the worms. 'It's a very kind offer, but I'll have to accept it some other time.'

Then he went over to Algy, who was throwing plasma twigs, obviously hoping the dog microbes would run and fetch them and stop jiggling on his lower tendrils.

They weren't.

'Come on, Algy,' said Wilton quietly. 'Let's find a way to get back onto our janet.'

'What do you reckon, Algy?' said Wilton. 'Can you do it?'

Algy peered into the dog's ear.

'I dunno,' he said. 'It looks very dark in there. And scary.'

Wilton hated asking Algy to go on such a dangerous mission, but he didn't have any choice.

'I'd go in myself,' he said, 'if I could.'

The worm who'd guided them to the dog's ear shook its front end. 'Don't even try it,' said the worm to Wilton. 'You won't get past the eardrum. Only a microbe can squeeze past and get to the brain.'

'If you don't want to go in there,' Wilton said to Algy, 'you don't have to. We'll think of something else.'

Algy peered into the ear again and shuddered.

Wilton knew how he felt. The thought of creeping into the dark depths of a strange ear made him shudder too.

'The basic task's a breeze,' said Algy. 'Making a host feel hungry is what we parasites do all the time. It's how we get most of our food. I've done it to you heaps.'

'I know,' said Wilton. 'That's how I got the idea.'

'What I still don't understand,' said Algy, 'is why I have to go in this end. Why can't I go in the usual end?'

'Too dangerous,' said Wilton.

'Pollution in the digestive system,' said the worm. 'Dog had a garbage bin lunch.'

'And it's much further to travel,' said Wilton. 'By the time you've reached the stomach and done whatever you do there to get the hunger juices flowing, our janet might have gone.'

Wilton peered out through the dog forest.

Their janet was still sitting in the distance, head in tendrils, but for how much longer?

'OK,' said Algy. 'I'll give it a go.'

Wilton's gratitude molecules swelled as he gazed at his friend.

'Explain once more about the drain,' Algy was saying to the worm.

'Not drain,' said the worm. 'Brain. Some living organisms don't have think molecules scattered through their bodies like us. They have theirs all bunched in one place inside their head. It's called their brain.'

'That's crazy,' said Algy. 'How do their bottoms think?'

'We don't have to worry about that now,' said Wilton. 'We just have to concentrate on getting to the dog's brain.'

'You mean I do,' said Algy.

'Yes,' said Wilton quietly. 'You do.'

Wilton waited on the dog's ear flap, rigid with worry.

'Algy's been gone ages,' he said. 'Something awful's happened.'

'Relax,' said the worm. 'He's probably just taking it slowly while he sneaks past the killer wax fungus.'

'Killer wax fungus?' squeaked Wilton. 'You didn't say anything about killer wax fungus.'

'Relax,' insisted the worm. 'Worrying isn't going to help him now.'

'I'm going in,' said Wilton. 'I'm not leaving him to face killer wax fungus on his own.'

The worm blocked his way.

'You won't fit,' said the worm. 'And killer wax fungus isn't that much of a problem. It can't move. It's trapped in the wax. The only way it can kill you is if you eat it.'

Great, thought Wilton. Algy meeting something he mustn't eat. Why don't I feel reassured?

Wilton tried to relax. But his think molecules were going bonkers. What if Algy got through, met some brain cells as planned, and then got into a violent argument with them about whether sludge gods exist or not?

Or what if he got lost and ended up in the dog's nose? There was probably killer snot fungus there, as well as killer nose hair fungus.

Or what if . . .

'That,' said a familiar voice, 'was the scariest thing I've ever done in my life. I'm starving.'

Wilton spun round, joy molecules bouncing off relief molecules all through him.

'Algy,' he said. 'Thank sludge you're safe.'

Algy was trudging out of the ear, tendrils drooping wearily at his side.

'How did you go?' asked the worm.

'Mission done,' said Algy. 'I met some brain cells like you said and explained our problem and they were very helpful. Said they'd be very happy to get the hunger molecules working. They reckon their dog doesn't get enough to eat anyway. All this talk of food has made me feel pretty hungry too. Luckily the brain cells warned me not to eat any wax on the way out.'

'Algy,' said Wilton, 'you're a legend.'

'Let's hope it works,' said Algy. He pointed to Wilton's tummy. 'OK if I pop inside for a feed?'

'Of course,' said Wilton.

If he had tendrils he would have given Algy a hug as well as a feed.

He saw Algy was hesitating.

'There was another reason I did it,' said Algy. 'Apart from the ones we discussed.'

He gave Wilton a steady squiz, and Wilton saw

that his tendrils weren't just weary, they were sad as well.

'What was it?' said Wilton.

'I just wanted to show you,' said Algy, 'that with us parasites, it's not all take, take, take.'

'I know that,' said Wilton softly.

But Algy had already disappeared.

Wilton crouched on the dog's head, none of his molecules moving.

Well, hardly any of them.

'Is it working?' said a voice.

Wilton could feel Algy peeking out of his rear entrance.

'Get back inside,' he hissed urgently. 'There's no point in it working at all if you get left behind.'

Algy went back inside.

Wilton peered ahead through the dog forest.

It was working. The dog was approaching their janet, who was sitting against a tree eating something dark and sticky-looking just as Wilton had hoped.

The janet was looking up, surprised. Now she was looking alarmed. Now she was looking not so alarmed.

Good on you, worms, thought Wilton.

They were obviously doing their job up the other end, making the dog's tail wag in a friendly way.

The janet was smiling.

The dog was licking her hand in an even more friendly way.

'Arghhh,' yelled Algy's voice. 'We're in the wrong place.'

Wilton realised the voice wasn't muffled. Algy was on his shoulder.

'Get back inside,' he said.

'He's licking her hand,' shrieked Algy. 'We shouldn't be on the head, we should be on the tongue.'

'Go back in,' insisted Wilton. 'It's under control. The worms said this would happen. Be patient. Our turn will come.'

Grumbling and complaining and predicting doom and failure, Algy went back inside.

For a few excruciating moments, Wilton feared he might be right.

Then, just as the worms had said, the janet reached out the end of her tendril and patted the dog on the head.

'We're on,' yelled Wilton. 'We're back on a finger. We're back on the janet.'

Algy appeared on Wilton's shoulder, looking delighted.

Wilton tried to feel delighted too. He did in a way, but as he waved goodbye with his tail to the worms on the dog's bottom, he also felt sad.

The worms were too far off to see clearly, but he knew they were waving back.

'See you,' Wilton called to them wistfully.

'Slithering sludge.'

Suddenly Algy was gripping him and sounding very alarmed.

'How are you doing this?' squeaked Algy. 'Keeping us on the finger when you haven't got any tendrils or plasma strands to cling on with and we're not wedged under a fingernail?'

Wilton nodded at the rough surface of the finger.

'See that dark stuff,' he said.

'What,' said Algy, 'the dark stuff clogging up the gullies and smeared over the ridges?'

'I think it's called chocolate,' said Wilton. 'The worms told me that janets often have sticky patches of it on their fingers. So when our janet started patting the dog's head, I spotted one and positioned us so we'd stick to it.'

'Brilliant,' said Algy. 'You're not just a long tube of eating opportunities.'

'Thanks,' said Wilton.

But he didn't feel brilliant. Not with what lay ahead.

The main problem was the sheer distance they had to travel to get back to the sludge tunnel. All the way up the tendril, down the entire surface of the janet to the underpants, and over at least one of those two huge round hills.

'And after all that way,' said Wilton to Algy, 'we still have to get back up the clogged and fungus-infested sludge tunnel to our valley.'

He felt weak at the thought, and a bit ill.

It all seemed overwhelming.

Who am I kidding, thought Wilton miserably. I'm just a worm. One puny little worm. How can I possibly help the poor janet when I'm this tiny?

He stared down at his body, which suddenly seemed smaller than it ever had before.

'We can do it,' said Algy. 'Together.'

Algy was staring at Wilton with a familiar expression. The same look of total belief he'd had when Wilton was tunnelling through the sludge blockage.

Now, seeing Algy's expression, Wilton felt his determination molecules lock together.

Good on you, Algy, he thought gratefully.

Algy might not be long and wriggly, but just how important was that in a friend? Wilton decided that later, when there was more time, he'd curl up and give Algy a hug.

'Thanks,' he said for now.

'That's OK,' said Algy. 'Your strength and my brains. Unbeatable.'

Wilton concentrated on getting the journey started. He wriggled hard until the sticky strands of chocolate under his tummy began to stretch and he was able to start moving slowly along the finger.

He hoped it wouldn't be this difficult all the way.

'Algy,' he said. 'It looks to me like most of the surface of the janet is covered in underpants. What do you reckon?'

Algy didn't reply. He'd disappeared.

Must be inside eating, thought Wilton.

He peered back over at the janet's main body section. It did seem to be covered in a layer of various types of underpants, bigger and looser and different colours, but definitely underpants.

'If we can get inside that outer layer,' said Wilton to his tummy, 'I reckon the going will be easier because we won't have to worry about falling off the surface of the janet. What do you reckon, Algy?'

Algy still didn't reply.

'Algy, are you eating?' called Wilton more loudly. He guessed Algy was, because he could feel some slightly unpleasant feelings inside.

'Yes,' called Algy's voice. 'It's delicious. You should try some.'

Algy's voice wasn't muffled and, Wilton realised, Algy wasn't on his shoulder either.

He looked around.

Close by were a cluster of bacteria feeding greedily in a chocolate-filled gully. Among them, chocolate molecules hanging off his tendrils, was Algy.

'Come and have some,' called Algy, waving enthusiastically. 'It's yummy.'

'No,' said Wilton sternly. 'We've got to get going.'

'But this'll give us energy for the journey home,' said Algy plaintively.

'Algy,' said Wilton. 'If the janet pats the dog again, we won't be going home because we'll be back on the dog.'

Algy thought about this. He gave one last longing squiz at the chocolate, then headed for Wilton's rear entrance.

'I'll be in here if you need me,' said Algy, disappearing.

Wilton felt a violent jolt. For a moment he thought Algy was rearranging things inside again. Then he realised that wasn't it.

The janet's tendril had started to hurtle through

outer space. Wilton pressed himself into the sticky chocolate strands so he wouldn't be flung off.

'What's happening?' squeaked Algy's muffled voice.

Wilton squizzed anxiously to see where the tendril was headed.

And relaxed.

It wasn't moving towards the dog.

Then he tensed again as he saw what it was moving towards.

A big blue shiny square spaceship.

'We're off the janet,' yelled Wilton. 'We're off the janet.'

Algy appeared on his shoulder, tendrils waving hysterically.

'What happened?' he squeaked. 'What happened?'

'I couldn't hang on,' said Wilton, sick with distress. 'The janet took the lid off the spaceship and we got knocked off the finger.'

They looked around at the shiny blue walls of the spaceship looming over them.

'What's a spaceship?' said Algy.

Wilton explained about the spaceship myths and legends and gossip he'd overheard from ancient slime patches.

'Though,' added Wilton, 'the spaceships the slime patches talked about were usually green and white capsules with molecules in them that cured headaches.'

'You're sure it was molecules?' asked Algy. 'Not paddocks?'

Wilton saw what Algy meant.

He and Algy were in a huge paddock. A white spongy paddock that crumbled as you wriggled over it and was full of caves and craters you had to be careful not to fall into.

In fact, Wilton saw as he peered over the edge, he and Algy were on a pile of paddocks. A white one on top of a green one on top of a yellow one on top of another white one. And so on, as far down as he could see.

'Slithering sludge,' said Algy. 'I've never seen a pile of paddocks before.'

'Don't be a jiffing idiot,' said a chocolate-covered bacteria scowling out of a crater. 'This isn't a pile of paddocks, you stupid ajax, it's a couple of cheese and lettuce sandwiches.'

Wilton stared at the bacteria.

'And while we're at it, handy andy,' said another bacteria to Wilton. 'This isn't a jiffing spaceship, it's a lunchbox.'

Wilton squizzed around, bewildered. And noticed for the first time a huge pink cliff face behind him covered in what looked horribly like worms the same as him, only dead.

'And that, harpic-for-brains, is a pink lamington,' said a third bacteria. 'Don't worry, they're not dead worms, that's coconut.'

Wilton tried to take all this in but it wasn't easy

because suddenly waves of nausea were rippling through him.

Must be stress, he thought. The stress and grief of saying goodbye to the dog worms and knowing I'll never see them again.

'What's a sandwich?' Algy was asking the first bacteria.

'Food, you dopey domestos,' it replied. 'It's one of the things our janet eats. That and chocolate.'

Even though he was dizzy with sickness, Wilton's think molecules spun into action.

Of course. Their janet had to eat just like every other living thing. Which answered the question philosophers and thinkers and slime patches had been debating since time began – where does sludge come from?

Wilton was still digesting this when the paddock started to move.

'The janet's picking it up,' squeaked Algy. 'She's picking up a sandwich. Quick, we can get back on her finger.'

'No,' yelled Wilton.

Through the mist of nausea, Wilton saw something clearly for the first time.

'The janet's got two entrance and exit places just like me,' he said. 'If she eats this sandwich with us on it, we can get home through her mouth, which'll be much quicker and easier than going all the way to the other entrance.'

'Brilliant,' said Algy.

'Pretty jiffing obvious if you ask us,' said the bacteria.

'There is just one problem,' said Algy.

'What's that?' asked Wilton.

All the bacteria started screaming and swearing. Wilton looked up in the direction Algy was pointing.

A huge wet open mouth was descending towards them.

The dog's mouth.

Wilton stared up at the black cavern of the dog's mouth. As it got bigger it blotted out most of the universe, including the pink lamington and the park next to the library.

'Howling harpic,' yelled the bacteria. 'Leg it everybody.'

Wilton couldn't leg it, but he could wriggle. As he struggled across the sandwich paddock, he felt the dog's hot hungry panting breath, close and getting closer.

He glanced up at the janet, far above, who was holding the sandwich out to the dog. Her face looked different now. Her eyes, instead of wet and scrunched, were bright and sparkling.

Good, thought Wilton. Someone's happy at least.

'Wriggle faster,' came Algy's muffled squeak. 'Wriggle faster.'

Wilton wriggled faster. He didn't waste energy

answering Algy. He was too busy thinking about the advice one of the chocolate-covered bacteria had given him before it dived into a sandwich crater.

'Watch out for the jiffing teeth.'

Very kind, thought Wilton, except I don't know what teeth are.

A huge globule of dog saliva splashed into the sandwich paddock near Wilton. It exploded into a spray of smaller globules, which battered Wilton like sludge chunks in a sludge storm.

Wilton peered up at the dog through the saliva rain. All he could see now were the dog's vast dripping jaws. Gleaming in the wet blackness were two rows of yellow mountains. The front ones had sharp pointed peaks.

Teeth.

Wilton had barely realised this when the teeth hurtled towards him. With a half-wriggle, half-spasm he flung himself backwards as the teeth plunged into the sandwich.

Just missing him.

Phew, thought Wilton, that was close.

Then the dog's lip flopped onto him, burying him under twenty-seven billion times his own body weight of slobbery skin.

That's what it felt like.

By the time Wilton had painfully wriggled out from under the lip, he expected to find himself in the dog's mouth.

But he wasn't. He was still on the sandwich. There was still hope.

Wilton surveyed the sandwich.

The dog's jaws were gripping one side of it. The janet's fingers were gripping the other side. They were both pulling.

The janet's face was glowing with what Wilton was now sure was happiness. The dog's eyes were glowing with what Wilton was equally sure was a desire to eat the whole sandwich, including him and Algy.

Hold on, Wilton begged the janet silently. For our sake and your sake, hold on.

The janet held on.

After a few more moments, the dog tossed its head and tore off its side of the sandwich.

Wilton, deafened by the alarmed curses of millions of bacteria, watched the dog gobble its mouthful down.

Don't give him any more, Wilton begged the janet. Have some yourself. You need the sludge.

He peered up at the janet's face. Oh no. She was gazing at the dog as if all she wanted in the whole of outer space was to feed this greedy mongrel more.

Just my luck, thought Wilton. My janet's the kindest, most generous janet in the whole universe and we're all going to be destroyed because of it.

Then a wonderful thing happened.

The janet licked her lips.

She opened her mouth.

She lifted the remains of the sandwich towards it.

'Yes,' shouted Wilton, relief molecules flooding through him. 'She's having some herself. We're saved.'

He wriggled as fast as he could over to the janet's side of the sandwich.

From inside Wilton's tummy came a muffled squeak.

'Watch out for the teeth.'

Wilton felt more ill than he ever had in his life.

It's not surprising really, he thought. I'm being swilled around in a great mouthful of cheese and lettuce and saliva and bacteria. Massive teeth mountains are trying to grind me into sludge. Lumps of soggy sandwich keep bouncing off me.

With a jolt of alarm, Wilton remembered Algy. He hadn't heard a squeak from Algy since the janet had bit into the sandwich and they'd found themselves in her mouth.

'Algy,' yelled Wilton. 'Are you OK?'

'Sort of,' called Algy's muffled voice. 'Hang on. I'll be out in a bit.'

Hang on to what? thought Wilton as he tried to swim away from the janet's huge tongue. Too late. The thrashing monster sent him spinning front over tail through a churning blizzard of sandwich lumps and swearing bacteria.

He managed to do a sideways wriggle just in time to avoid several teeth as they thundered together.

But only just.

What's happening to me? wondered Wilton. I can understand the headache and the body ache and the tail ache, that's just stress and grief, but why am I so weak and slow?

It was all he could do to stop himself being sucked into the massive whirlpool at the back of the mouth. He knew the whirlpool tunnel was the way home, but he just didn't feel up to going down there yet.

What I need, thought Wilton, is somewhere to rest for a while and get my strength back.

But where could a worm rest in a place like this?

Wilton was just starting to feel despairing as well as very crook when he saw a welcome sight. A cavity in one of the teeth, almost exactly the same size as the neighbours' cave at home.

Wriggling into it wasn't easy because of the spinning lumps of sandwich whizzing past and the swirling saliva dragging at him. Finally, though, Wilton managed to squeeze himself inside.

He flopped back, hurting all over.

'Algy,' he called weakly. 'Are you OK?'

'Actually,' called Algy's muffled voice, 'there's something I have to tell you. I'll be out in a moment.'

Wilton waited, the pain and weakness getting worse.

A horrible thought hit him. Was all this sickness just his body trying to tell him it didn't want to be here inside the janet? That it didn't want to go back to a place where nobody liked it and everyone called it fat?

Could be, thought Wilton miserably. Whatever it is, I can't ever imagine feeling worse than this.

Then he saw Algy, and he did.

'Algy', he gasped. 'What's happened to you?'

Algy was dishevelled and bruised and had bits missing from his ectoplasm.

'You poor thing,' said Wilton. 'Did you get bashed around in there while I was being tossed around in the saliva?'

'Yeah,' said Algy, dragging himself painfully up onto Wilton's shoulder. 'I got bashed around. But not by the saliva.'

'What then?' said Wilton.

Algy hesitated, and Wilton could see there was something his little friend was having trouble saying. He went to reassure Algy, to remind him there was nothing best friends couldn't say to each other, but before he could get the words out another spasm of pain and sickness twisted through him.

'Algy,' he whispered. 'What is it?'

'Remember when you were being a bridge?' said Algy.

'Yes,' said Wilton. 'Why?'

He'd never heard Algy sound so miserable or concerned.

'Remember how we thought we escaped from the killer fungus?' said Algy.

Suddenly Wilton felt so weak he couldn't even reply.

'Some fungus spores must have sneaked inside you and hidden themselves,' said Algy. 'They're in there now, multiplying, and I don't know how to stop them.'

Wilton shuddered.

The sick dizziness was getting worse.

He wasn't sure if it was from hearing Algy's terrible news or because the killer fungus inside him was already starting to destroy his molecules.

Both probably.

'Hold on, Wriggles,' Algy was saying on his shoulder. 'I'm going to get help.'

Wilton felt panic on top of everything else.

'Algy,' he said. 'You can't go off on your own. It's murder out there in that saliva. There are huge chunks of unrestrained cheese and vicious tidal currents and a tongue without any respect for life.'

Wilton tried to wriggle into a circle to somehow stop his friend from going, but it was no good – the tooth cavity was too small and he was too weak. And, he realised with another anguished shudder, Algy couldn't even take refuge inside him. Not with the fungus in there.

'It's OK,' Algy was saying. 'I'm not frightened.'

'Don't be silly,' said Wilton gently. 'You're allowed to be frightened. I don't blame you. I've been frightened by a lot of things on this trip and I'm much bigger than you. If I was as tiny as you I'd probably be trying to hide up my own food tube right now.'

Wilton wasn't sure if he was making sense. He was too sick to think straight.

Algy wasn't saying anything. Wilton could see he was embarrassed.

'While I've been hanging out inside you,' mumbled Algy, 'I've been borrowing a few molecules. Including some bravery ones.'

Wilton stared at Algy.

In among the weakness and the nausea, he felt a surge of relief and pride.

'Good on you, Algy,' he said. 'I'm glad you've got them. I'd much rather you have them instead of them being destroyed along with all the others by that mean vicious fungus.'

'Don't even say that,' replied Algy.

'Too late,' croaked Wilton, confused. 'I just did.'

'I'm going to get help,' said Algy. 'Hang on. I'll be back soon.'

Wilton lost track of time.

'Algy,' he called at one point. 'Algy.'

There was no reply.

Wilton remembered that Algy had leapt onto a

passing lump of cheese to go and get help.

That was ages ago.

What was ages ago?

Wilton struggled to think straight. Why couldn't he think straight?

A spasm of pain went through him and he remembered why. His think molecules were being choked by mean vicious killer fungus spores without a kind molecule in their bodies.

Not like Algy.

He's got loads of kind molecules in his body, thought Wilton. And not just ones he's borrowed from me. Algy is the kindest microbe in the whole universe.

'Do you hear me?' he shouted weakly at a passing swarm of enzymes. 'The kindest microbe in the whole universe.'

The enzymes didn't seem to hear him. Wilton realised it was because they were bits of cheese.

He didn't care.

'The kindest microbe in the whole universe,' he repeated to the cheese.

That's why, thought Wilton a short time afterwards, or perhaps it was a long time, that's why I'll understand if Algy doesn't come back. It won't be because he's unkind. It'll just be common sense.

Algy's a parasite, thought Wilton a bit or a lot later.

Like me.

We parasites need a healthy host.

It's OK, Algy, I'll understand if you don't come back.

Thank you for being my friend.

'Wriggles, wake up.'

Wilton struggled to work out where the voice was coming from.

'Wake up, Wriggles, please.'

Then he realised.

His shoulder.

'Algy,' he tried to say, but the pain was too great.

It was Algy. And he seemed to have an army with him. Battalions of tiny warriors. And one bigger companion, a lady with the sort of intelligent expression on her cell wall that made Wilton think she'd be very good at solving the dopey riddles slime patches came up with when they were bored, which was most of the time because their attempts to play soccer were pretty pathetic and . . .

'Wriggles,' said Algy urgently. 'Stay with us. These are white blood cells from our janet's immune system. They've kindly agreed to help us with our fungus problem. And this lady's a brain cell. She's from the part of our janet's brain that manages the immune system. She's here to supervise the operation.'

Wilton struggled to take all this in.

'What operation?' he asked feebly.

'Don't worry about it,' said Algy. 'We're going to make you better.'

'Thank you,' said Wilton. He wanted to say more, to tell Algy he was the best friend in the whole universe, but his chat molecules were in a bad way.

'Young worm,' said the brain cell.

Wilton realised she was speaking to him.

'Do we have your permission for an entry?' said the brain cell.

'Yes,' whispered Wilton. He wasn't exactly sure what she meant, but anything that was all right with Algy was all right with him.

The brain cell started ordering the white blood cells to proceed to Wilton's entrance points.

Wilton managed a final couple of words to Algy.

'Be careful.'

Algy held his tendrils out wide.

'Hey,' he said softly, 'when am I not careful? I'm so careful that in dangerous battle situations, I even take a spare.'

Wilton didn't have a clue what Algy was on about.

Then he saw that Algy's ectoplasm was stretching out of shape, and his nucleus was ... pine-o-clean, was this possible? ... dividing into two, and his whole body was twisting, splitting, separating ...

... into two identical Algys.

The two Algys finally separated with a loud pop. The sound reminded Wilton of being on his ledge long ago, gazing down into the valley and hearing popping noises in the distance and not knowing what they were.

He did now.

'Sorry you had to see that,' said the Algys. 'We microbes prefer to do that in private, but this is an emergency. Try to relax, and we'll have you better before you can say "tickle me".'

Wilton stared at the two Algys, astounded, delighted, praying his squiz molecules weren't as crook as his chat ones.

Two best friends were even better than one.

The Algys touched him tenderly on the shoulder with their tendrils.

'See you soon,' they said.

Wilton was amazed how quickly he started to feel better.

Soon the pain and sickness were almost gone. Even his skin, which had been burning where it touched the inside of the tooth cavity, was cool again.

'Good on you, Algy,' Wilton called out gratefully.

Algy didn't reply. Wilton wasn't surprised.

Probably can't hear me over the din of the battle, he thought.

It had been a big battle. Wilton's body had bulged in all sorts of odd places. He'd experienced the sort of tremors and convulsions and twitches that he guessed could only be caused by huge internal troop movements. Some of the skirmishes had almost flipped him out of the tooth cavity.

But now there was very little movement.

The battle must be almost over.

He couldn't hear battle sounds any more. Not even the squeak of dying fungus spores. They must all be dead. That's why he was feeling so good.

And it was all thanks to Algy.

Wilton was filled with so much gratitude he couldn't stop himself. He called out to a swarm of passing cheese fragments, 'Algy's the best friend in the whole universe.'

The cheese fragments didn't respond, but the enzymes on them waved to Wilton and cheered.

Wilton felt like cheering too, because suddenly the saliva around him was full of white blood cells emerging from his rear exit and forming up into their platoons and squadrons.

There were less of them than had gone in, Wilton noticed, but they carried themselves like victors.

'Thank you,' said Wilton. 'Thank you all very much.'

He was deeply grateful. But he was also starting to feel the first tiny stabs of anxiety.

'Algy,' he called. 'Algy, where are you? Come out and get a medal.'

The brain cell emerged.

Alone.

'Where's Algy?' asked Wilton.

The brain cell seemed not to hear. She started dismissing the white blood cells, who sped away through the saliva, relieved to be off-duty. Within moments they were partying with the enzymes on the cheese fragments.

Wilton didn't feel relieved.

Panic was building inside him.

Until he had a thought. Of course. What would be the one thing Algy would do after an energetic and draining battle?

Eat.

Wilton slumped back into the tooth cavity, tingling with relief.

'Take your time,' he called to his tummy. 'Both of you.'

The brain cell finished dismissing the troops and turned to Wilton.

'Mission accomplished, young worm,' she said. 'Fungus engaged and destroyed.'

'Thank you,' said Wilton. 'I'm very grateful to you and your troops.'

'You should also be grateful to your friend,' said the brain cell. 'He's a hero.'

'I know,' said Wilton. 'I'm very lucky to have a friend like Algy.' He raised his voice to a cheery yell. 'Even if both the guzzle-guts are eating me out of house and home.'

'Unfortunately,' said the brain cell, 'he can't hear you.'

Oh no, thought Wilton. I hope his noise molecules weren't damaged in the battle.

'Your friend didn't make it,' said the brain cell.

Wilton stared at her, think molecules scrambled, desperately hoping he'd misunderstood.

'Didn't make ... what?' said Wilton.

'He was killed,' said the brain cell.

Wilton tried to speak for a long time, but he couldn't.

'Both . . . both of him?' he whispered finally.

'Yes,' said the brain cell. 'They both fought hard and bravely, and I don't think we'd have achieved victory without them. At the height of the battle the fungus attacked us from behind. Your friend held them off until we could regroup. He went down fighting. And, if I remember correctly, arguing.'

Wilton wished the nausea and migraine and painful skin would come back, a hundred times as strong, to blot out what he was feeling now.

'There is some good news,' said the brain cell.

Wilton barely heard her.

How could any news be good?

'I'm getting reports from our optical division,' said the brain cell. 'They're saying that our host organism, Janet, has made friends with a stray dog. This is reducing her stress levels wonderfully. Already our weather division is monitoring far fewer storms and food processing disruptions.'

Dimly, painfully, Wilton realised this must be a good thing.

But he didn't really care.

The brain cell turned to go.

'I'll leave you with your thoughts,' she said.

Wilton curled up in the tooth cavity and thought about Algy.

His generosity.

His bravery.

His kindness and considerateness in only choosing non-essential bits of Wilton to eat.

The thought of not having Algy around was more than Wilton could bear. No more Algy grinning on his shoulder. No more Algy scampering down to his rear entrance. No more Algy coming up with very brilliant slightly muffled suggestions from his tummy.

Please, begged Wilton, please don't let him be dead.

But he was.

Huge fat worm sobs shuddered through Wilton. Misery molecules filled every part of him, including his food tube.

Anyone who doesn't have a parasite like Algy living inside them, thought Wilton, is a sad person indeed.

Then, much later, Wilton slowly started thinking about other things.

He was glad the janet had made friends with the dog. He was glad she was getting better. He hoped she carried on getting better after he left.

Which he planned to do as soon as he could.

Wilton knew it was the only way the misery of losing Algy would ever get less painful.

He had to leave the janet.

When the brain cell came back, Wilton was still in the tooth cavity trying to get directions from passers-by.

'If I can find my way to an eye-socket,' he was saying to a group of bacteria, 'I can get back onto a finger when the janet rubs her eye and back to the worms when she pats the dog.'

'Eye-socket?' said one of the bacteria. It turned to the others. 'Anyone know how this dopey napisan can get to an eye-socket?'

The other bacteria all shrugged.

'I can point you to the tonsils,' said the first bacteria, 'but after that your jiffing guess is as good as mine.'

'Thanks anyway,' said Wilton.

This is hopeless, he thought as the bacteria swirled away. No one seems to know.

'Young worm,' said a voice.

Wilton looked up and saw the brain cell regarding him coolly.

'Regarding our earlier conversation,' she said. 'There is one more piece of bad news I didn't mention.'

Wilton could see she was going to mention it now, even though what he really wanted to talk about was the shortest route to an eye-socket as the worm wriggles.

'Our host organism is recovering,' continued the brain cell, 'but she has a long way to go. There are still areas of fungus infestation in the stomach and small intestine. Including your home valley.'

Wilton looked at her.

He could tell she was trying to make a point,

but his grieving think molecules didn't want to grasp it.

'The killer fungus armies get their nutrition from stress toxins,' the brain cell went on. 'The microbes in the stomach and intestine are capable of neutralising the toxins and starving the fungus, but the trouble is they don't know the toxins are there.'

'Why don't you tell them?' said Wilton.

'We can't get a message through,' said the brain cell. 'The fungus is hampering our communication systems.'

'Why don't you go down and tell the stomach microbes yourself?' said Wilton.

'We intelligence operatives can't function in digestive juices,' said the brain cell. 'Only organisms with acid-proof skin can do that. Skin like yours.'

Now Wilton understood.

'Is this why you saved me?' he asked quietly. 'When Algy asked for your help, is this why you agreed?'

The brain cell's expression didn't change.

'Yes,' she said.

Wilton looked at her, squiz molecules to squiz molecules.

'My best friend has just died,' he said. 'I'm not really in the mood for intelligence work.'

The brain cell's expression still didn't change.

'The fate of our world depends on you,' she said.

She doesn't get it, thought Wilton.

'I'm a worm,' said Wilton. 'I don't belong in this janet. They hate me here, they always have. They call me names and make me stay on a ledge with a grumpy patch of slime.'

The brain cell didn't say anything.

She still doesn't get it, thought Wilton.

He wished Algy was around to help explain it to her.

Except Algy wouldn't be hanging around explaining stuff. He'd be inside Wilton's food tube, pleading with Wilton to get a wriggle on so they could save the janet.

Muffled and hungry and indignant, but prepared to risk everything.

Wilton suddenly felt such a huge pang of love for Algy, even a big body like his couldn't keep it all inside.

'OK,' he said quietly. 'I'll do it.'

The worst part was waiting for the janet to eat another sandwich.

Finally, she did.

Wilton wriggled out of the tooth cavity, tunnelled into a soggy ball of bread and cheese and lettuce and waited for the janet's tongue to send him plummeting down her throat.

He peeked out.

'Here it comes,' he said to himself, struggling to control his panic as the tongue headed for him.

He thought of Algy. The memory made Wilton's food tube feel painfully empty, but it also helped him feel less scared.

Just a bit.

The writhing tongue monster seemed to fill the entire mouth for a moment, sending a tidal wave of saliva and food chunks and partying enzymes sluicing into the dark hole of the throat tunnel.

And Wilton.

He huddled deeper into the mashed sandwich and prayed the brain cell was right. She'd told him that food didn't just drop down the throat tunnel and smash into the stomach in an explosion of startled molecules. She'd promised that he and his sandwich sludge would be carried gently down the tunnel by rippling muscular movements and that he'd arrive in the stomach relaxed and refreshed.

She was partly right.

Wilton peeked out again and saw he wasn't plummeting, which was refreshing and slightly relaxing.

But he wasn't able to relax too much because of what else he saw. Armies of white blood cells on the throat muscles locked in desperate battle with armies of frenzied fungus.

Wilton wriggled inside the sludge again and tried not to think about what might be waiting for him at home.

A valley crawling with fungus.

Algy's family all dead and in pieces.

The neighbours so bloated with fungus spores living inside them that they couldn't even fit into their cave.

Please let me be in time, thought Wilton.

The sandwich sludge gave a sudden violent jolt and Wilton slid out.

He saw he'd arrived.

This had to be the stomach because of its sheer size. It was more of a cave than a valley, but its vastness made every other cave Wilton had ever seen look smaller than a dimple on an amoeba's bum.

Wilton realised he was swimming in acid.

He felt his skin starting to burn.

Jeepers, he thought, this is strong stuff.

He wriggled up onto a nodule, which gave him an acid-free vantage point to look out across the stomach.

It was an incredible squiz. On countless other nodules, groups of microbes were on duty at natural springs, aiming squirts of acid at lumps of food sludge dropping down from the delivery tunnel.

Not many of the microbes were concentrating completely on their work.

Most were throwing anxious glances at the walls of the stomach where, despite the valiant efforts of the white blood cell armies, the fungus hordes were relentlessly advancing.

Wilton saw another tunnel running out of the back of the stomach.

From the colour and texture of the sludge running into it, and the familiar weary expression on the faces of the enzymes sprawled on the sludge, Wilton guessed what was at the other end of the tunnel.

His valley.

Oh no.

Platoons of white blood cells were only just

managing to hold seething waves of fungus back from the tunnel entrance.

Wilton could see they wouldn't be able to for much longer.

He had to act now.

'Excuse me, everyone,' he said.

Nobody so much as paused or looked up.

Wilton realised what the problem was. Nervousness was making his chat molecules seize up. In the clamour of everything that was going on, not a single microbe had heard his feeble squeak.

Come on, Wilton told himself sternly. There's nothing to be nervous about.

But there was.

Everyone probably calling him names, for a start, and perhaps getting angry that he was back, and maybe even jeering at him for being such a pathetic public speaker.

Wilton thought of Algy, and how brave one of the smallest microbes in the whole janet had been.

He pulled himself together.

'Excuse me, everyone,' he shouted in a voice so loud he surprised even himself. 'I've got something important to tell you.'

This time he had almost everyone's attention. Not the armies, but the workers and the supervisors and most of the bacteria.

'Slithering sludge,' muttered a worker. 'That is the fattest microbe I've ever seen.'

'I'm not a microbe,' said Wilton. 'I'm a worm.'

'You're still fat,' said the worker.

Wilton ignored this and carried on.

'I know what's causing the fungus invasions,' he said. 'And the storms and the sick sludge and the tunnel blockages.'

'So do we, you big ajax,' said a bacteria. 'The sludge gods are angry. Everyone jiffing knows that.'

'It's not the sludge gods,' said Wilton.

The workers and supervisors and bacteria stared at him for a moment, then burst out laughing.

'Listen to me,' pleaded Wilton. 'I've been to outer space and I've seen the truth. We live in a giant janet and she's a bit plump and the other kids are cruel to her and she's very stressed. But don't worry. She's made friends with a dog and things are looking better as long as we do our bit.'

The entire stomach went silent, except for the distant sound of fungus gobbling up white blood cells.

Then the laughter started again, much louder.

'Poor harpic,' shouted another bacteria. 'Not only is he a worm, he's an idiot.'

'Get lost, lardboy,' growled a supervisor, waving his tendrils threateningly. 'We've got too many problems here to waste time listening to a loony.'

'Outer space,' scoffed the workers and supervisors and bacteria as they went back to work. 'There's no such jiffing thing.'

'Wait,' yelled Wilton. 'I can prove there is.'

A few of the microbes glanced back at him.

Wilton pointed to the lumps of sludge dropping out of the delivery tunnel.

'See how the incoming sludge is green and yellow and white?' he said. 'That's because it's a cheese and lettuce sandwich. It's what janets eat.'

The microbes turned away again, muttering things like 'fatso' and 'nutso'.

'In a while,' yelled Wilton, 'the incoming sludge will be pink with white bits in it. They'll look like dead worms, but they'll actually be coconut.'

Most of the microbes ignored him.

'You're the coconut,' muttered one.

Wilton waited, praying that when the janet finished her sandwich she'd move on to the lamington.

He remembered how Algy always used to put his tendrils on his hips when he was making a point. Wilton wished he had tendrils, and hips, so he could do the same.

He didn't, so he just waited.

And waited.

The fungus hordes, he saw, were about to pour down the exit tunnel into his valley.

Then a cry went up from the other side of the stomach.

'Look. Pink sludge. With jiffing white bits in it.'

Wilton peered up at the delivery tunnel, weak with relief.

Soggy lumps of pink lamington were plopping into the stomach.

It was only when Wilton stopped gazing at the lamington that he realised every worker, every supervisor and every microbe in the entire stomach was gazing at him.

Awe-struck.

Those whose tendrils had knee-joints were kneeling.

'Forgive us,' cried one, 'O wise and mighty worm god. Show us what we must do to save the world.'

'Yes,' they all cried. 'We beg you, O worshipful worm god. Tell us how to save the janet.'

Wilton stared at them, stunned.

He started to explain that he wasn't a god, just a worm trying to help.

Then he changed his mind.

It felt quite nice being worshipped for a change, plus it meant everyone would pay attention when he explained to them about the stress toxins and how to give the fungus the flick.

After Wilton explained to everyone about the stress toxins and how to give the fungus the flick, and they did, he got fed up with being worshipped.

He decided to go home.

Let's hope, thought Wilton as he wriggled down the tunnel to his valley, they don't carry on like that there as well.

They did.

A mighty roar went up as Wilton emerged from the tunnel.

'Good on you, Wilton,' yelled countless voices. 'You're a legend.'

The gleaming healthy sludge paddocks and the verdant valley slopes were covered with workers and farmers and viruses and enzymes, all waving and cheering.

'Welcome home, Wilton,' they yelled.

The ancient farmer came forward and clasped Wilton with trembling tendrils.

'Wilton,' he said. 'We used to think you were a fat dope. We were wrong, lad. You're a hero and a credit to worms everywhere. To show our everlasting gratitude to you for saving us from the fungus, I have the proud honour to hereby bestow on you the freedom of the valley.'

'Wil-ton,' roared the crowds and flocks in fervent delight. 'Wil-ton, Wil-ton, Wil-ton.'

Wilton looked at them all.

He knew he should be grateful and delighted. But he felt too sad, seeing the valley again.

This is Algy's home as well, thought Wilton. He saved it just as much as me. I wish he was here to get thanked too.

To be hailed as a hero.

To be given the freedom of the valley.

To be my friend.

Wilton struggled with his feelings. This wasn't the time for worm sobs. Blubbing here would just make everyone else upset.

Wilton realised the cheers were dying away. The crowds and flocks were going silent.

I'm spoiling their party, thought Wilton.

But he couldn't help it. They might as well get used to seeing him like this because this was how he'd always be.

The saddest worm in the world.

'Hey, Wriggles,' said a familiar voice.

'Aren't you going to say g'day?' said another familiar voice.

'Too big and important for us, eh?' said a third familiar voice.

Wilton wriggled around.

Staring at him, tendrils on hips, ectoplasm beaming, was Algy.

Two Algys.

A crowd of Algys.

Wilton stared in shock and amazement.

'But,' he stammered, 'aren't you ... aren't you ...?'

'Dead?' said one of the Algys.

'Only a couple of us,' said another.

'Remember our motto?' said another. 'About never going into dangerous situations without a spare? Well the first Algy was pretty sure hanging around inside you wasn't going to be a tea party all the time, so before he left home to join you on the journey, he made a few copies.'

Wilton curled himself into a big delighted circle, hugging his best friend in the whole janet.

Or rather, he thought happily, his best friends.

He could hardly wait to tell them about all the adventures they'd been having, and how they'd been into outer space and visited other janets, and how brave they were even though they might not know it yet.

The onlookers started cheering again. Wilton gave them a grateful look. And saw, in the crowd, more familiar faces.

The neighbours.

In fact, Wilton saw as he wriggled his tail at them delightedly, there seemed to be quite a few neighbours as well.

Hope they've got a bigger cave, he thought.

'Hey, Wriggles,' said the Algys. 'We've got a prezzie for you. Just came down in the sludge.'

The Algys parted to reveal a familiar round object.

Well, sort of familiar. Wilton had never seen a whole one before, only a half. And he'd never seen one unhatched like this.

'A worm egg,' whispered Wilton. 'Thank you.'

It was the best present he'd ever been given.

'Our theory,' said the Algys, 'is that the janet picked it up patting the dog. We thought you might like having another worm around.'

'Yes,' said Wilton as he stroked the egg. 'I'd like that very much.'

He gave his best friends another hug.

Then he looked up at the valley slopes.

He felt like wriggling up and rolling back down, just for fun.

Join Limpy the cane toad in three hilarious, heroic adventures

TOAD RAGE TOAD HEAVEN TOAD AWAY

From the Sydney Olympics to the Amazon jungle, Limpy just can't help getting into some sticky situations.

Be warned – it could get messy!

'A hilarious high-speed read . . . a real ripper!'
– *Sunday Times*

puffin.co.uk

morrisgleitzman.com

Teacher's Pet

'Ginger, Ginger, Ginger,' said Mr Napier. 'How did a nice family like yours end up with a person like you in it?'

Trouble seems to follow Ginger around, especially as her best friend is a fierce-looking stray dog.

'Morris Gleitzman has a rare gift for writing very funny stories'
- *Guardian*

'Readers can't get enough of him'
- *Independent*

Two Weeks with the Queen

Colin Mudford is on a
quest. His brother,
Luke, has cancer and
the doctors in
Australia don't seem
to be able to cure
him. Colin reckons
it's up to him to
find the best
doctor in the
world.

How better to do this than
asking the Queen to help . . .?

'A gem of a book' - *Guardian*

'One of the best books I've ever read.
I wish I had written it' - Paula Danziger

puffin.co.uk

morrisgleitzman.com

Angus daydreams of being a pirate – anything to take his mind off his mum's love life. Because, in the end, Angus always has to pick up the pieces . . .

Shortlisted for the Guardian Children's Fiction Award and the Carnegie Medal

'The most funny, truthful and affecting book I've read for some time. I began it with delight and finished it laughing aloud. It's a joy'

– Philip Pullman, author of the **His Dark Materials** trilogy

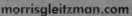